Before There Was a King Arthur

By

S.M. Cowan

Cover Design by: Author Laura Wright LaRoche
Contact her at: www.LLPIx.com or LLPix Designs.

1: The Beginning

Before there was the "Legend of King Arthur", there was another story of things that happened and one of the people who had helped lay the foundation, so he could come into power. This is the Legend of Queen Kieris, the woman that prepared things so Arthur could become King.

It is her story that I am going to tell you first. There once was an island named Hurricane. The people had named it that, because of the many storms that came in off the ocean and crossed the island. This island had several different kinds of shops, with the most skilled artisans, because this medium sized island was on the way to and from the bigger islands; many ships would stop to pick up things that they could sell somewhere else. On this island lived a family of weapon makers. Joshua and his wife Chasity made the finest swords and spears anywhere in the known world.

Chasity also had a brother named Joshua, but she called him Josh, so no one would get confused about whom she was talking to or about. Josh also lived on the island and was a maker of bows, arrows, and staffs. Joshua and his wife Chasity had two boys and she was expecting her third child any day. They had named the boys, Archer and Bowen. Even though they were twins, they were not identical. The boys were very smart and learned quickly. Their uncle Josh had been teaching them, how to make bows and arrows.

The boys were only four years old, when they each made their first weapons, without help from anyone. They were excited, and each took their weapon to show their parents. Bowen had made a very strange crooked looking bow. Archer had made some crooked arrows. The bow was light weight and easy for the boys to pull and shoot. Even at the age of four, both boys were really good shots, with a bow and arrow; hitting anything they targeted. Archer's arrows for some reason could not be shot in Bowen's bow but the boys had no trouble shooting them in any other bow. Their father took the bow and tried to shoot it. He also took one of the arrows, put it into another bow and tried to shoot it and could not shoot either. Chasity also tried when she saw how easily that the boys had shot them, but the crooked bow and crooked arrows could not be shot by anyone, other than Bowen or Archer. Their parents knew that these had to be magical weapons. They told the boys that they were special and that they should never sell them; but if they ever found someone, who could use the two of them together, then they should give the weapons to that person.

Joshua started teaching his boys how to hold a sword by letting them practice with pieces of wood shaped like swords. The wooden swords were light enough for them to handle without hurting themselves; but still learn some of the basic techniques. Chasity made spears for them that were just the right size for them to handle but left off the sharp metal points, so they would not accidently hurt each other as they learned how to use them. She was teaching them how to use them, so they could defend themselves. At four and a half years of age, both boys had mastered some of the easier basics of sword play and handling a spear; but they liked shooting their bows more than anything else, so that is what they practiced with the most. They both could shoot any bow and hit anything they aimed at. They were evenly matched and could not beat each other, unless one would shoot at the same target after the other. The last one to shoot would always win as he would split the other's arrow.

It would soon be the boys fifth birthday and Chasity's brother had been talking about taking the boys with him, when they turned five and opening a shop in a neighboring country. This new country was a large island country that lay about one hundred miles across a channel of water that was between them. He would take the swords, and spears which his sister and brother in law had made with him, sell them, and send the money back to them. The boys would go live and work for him in his shop, to pay their own way. He too had made the boys staffs and taught them how to use them for protection. Chasity hated to see the boys go, but they were not making enough money to feed and care for them, so she agreed to let them go. That would help them have enough to care for the new child, who would be born soon. She knew that they would be safe and well cared for by her brother. Josh, Bowen, and Archer left for the new land, on the boy's fifth birthday. Two days later, Chasity gave birth to a little girl. She was so beautiful with her red hair and big eyes. She could melt even the coldest heart is what one of the neighbors had said, when she stopped by to check on Chasity. Chasity loved her boys with all her heart, but she was so happy to finally have a little girl, she felt like her family was now complete.

Chasity's brother, Josh, opened his shop on the shore of the new country, as soon as they arrived. Besides crafting their art of bow and arrow making, their uncle Josh began to teach them more about how to use a sword, spear, and staff. He thought it was important that the boys could defend themselves in close quarters not just far away because on the weekends and late at night it could get pretty rough here. Before the boys turned six, they had become the finest bow and arrow makers, known anywhere. People would travel from great distances, even other countries just to buy what the boys had made.

Word came that a plague had hit the island of Hurricane and killed everyone. The boys never knew if they had another brother or a sister who died there with their parents. Their uncle made the boys a practice dummy to use their swords, spears, and staffs on. Right now, the boys only imagined the dummy was the plague, because they were missing their mom and dad so much. After the boys wore themselves out, they went to sleep. Then Josh had a turn at the dummy too. He could not let the boys see how upset he was over losing his sister and her husband. By the time Josh was through, the dummy was splintered and broken, only good for kindling for the fire. He would have to make them a new one in the morning. The last time they heard from their parents, Joshua and Chasity had reminded and warned the boys again, not to sell the strange bow and arrows that they had made. That this strange bow and arrows were magical, that they should be given to the first person, who could use both of them together. They also told them that they were doing ok, loved, and missed them. After some time and many wooden practice dummies, all three of them started to deal with losing Chasity and Joshua.

The boys would put on shooting demonstrations, to show how good that their bows and arrows were. They would even use, the strange looking ones, once in a while. They still could not shoot the crooked arrows in the crooked bow. When you put them together, the bow became heavy and you could not even pull the string back far enough to shoot it. Some people tried to buy them, just to hang on their walls but they were not for sale. Bowen and his brother Archer were born in 1802. Since age 4, Archer and Bowen could both hit anything they aimed at and thus had been banned from shooting in any of the tournaments, along the shore line. They had become so good at bow shooting, that no one else wanted to shoot against them, because no one was able to beat them. They never knew, what made the strange looking bow and strange looking arrows special. Maybe, it was just because these were the very first ones, which they had made without their uncle's help and that alone, made them special to the boys. The strange arrows did look good in Bowen's crooked bow. They still remembered their final words and warning to them about the bow and arrows.

They had crossed the ocean into the country with their uncle when they were five and still lived with him when they turned eighteen. For their eighteenth birthday, their uncle made them a birthday cake and gave them papers making them equal partners in the shop. They had worked so hard and had helped build up the business so much; their uncle thought they deserved it. He also had a surprise for them.

Josh: Boys, along with the last letter we received from your parents, they had also sent gifts for each of you, with a note that said for me to give them to you when the time was right. I feel you both have become mature responsible young men.

Josh left and came back with a wooden box. Josh: Here, there is a letter with it. The boys took the box from their uncle and sat it on the table. The box was very heavy; they looked at each other and opened it together. Inside the box were two swords, two spears and a letter. They left the weapons in the box to start with, because they were more interested in what their parents had said in the letter. They opened it together, first thing they noticed was, it was written in two different kinds of handwriting. They turned it around to show their uncle.

Josh: I see, both of them wrote the letter together for you. The curvy slightly slanted words are your mom's handwriting. The bold straight up and down words are your dad's handwriting.

The boys turned the letter back around and looked at it. Bowen: They both wrote it to us, so why don't we both read it together out loud.

Archer: Okay, that way uncle Josh will know what is says too, in case we have any questions. Bowen, you read mom's words and I will read dad's.

Bowen cleared his throat and began to read: My dear boys. I hope you are happy and well.

Archer: Even though you have not been gone long, we both miss you very much.

Bowen: Please don't be mad at your uncle for keeping this from you. I asked him to wait for the right time before he gave it to you.

Archer: The day you were born was the happiest day of our lives. On that day, a large rock fell out of the sky, next to our home.

Bowen: It turned out that the rock was made up of a special metal. Your weapons are made out of that metal.

Archer: The metal ended up being magical. It will not break, rust, or change shape after it has been cooled. We went through a few pieces before we figured out that we could not reheat it if we didn't like the shape of it.

Bowen: This means, that the swords will never break, rust, or get dull. The cores of these shafts and points of these spears are made of this metal too.

Archer: That means, it is stronger, won't warp or break. Keep these with you always, they will keep you safe.

Bowen: Tell your uncle, I said thank you, and that we miss him too. Love you both, always Mom and Dad.

None of them could speak for several moments, just taking in what they had said and who said it. The boys looked at each other and then at their uncle, who could not look up at them. They went over to their uncle and they both gave him a hug. Archer: Uncle, we don't hold anything against you. In fact, we appreciate everything you have done for us all these years.

Josh finally looked up: I am so glad; I don't think that I could handle it, if you ever got upset with me and left. You two are all the family that I have left now. They hugged him again.

Bowen: Uncle.

Josh: Yes, Bowen.

Bowen: Mom said that she loved you, too. And mom and dad both missed you.

Josh: I miss them too, but as long as you boys are around I will always have a part of my sister and her husband with me.

They hugged each other again and then the boys went back over to the box, to check out their weapons. On the swords, one of them had a B on the handle and the other one had an A on its handle. The spears also had a B on one and the other one had an A on it, both were next to the top of the blade of the spear.

The weapons were both just the right weight for each of them and was perfectly balanced.

Josh: I knew about the weapons but never saw them finished until your parents sent them here. They started working on them, on the day you were born. They had tried to finish them before we left. They thought when the big rock landed that it was a sign that you two would do something very important. Then when you two made the bow and arrow, they were sure and knew you would need these weapons to protect you on your quest.

Bowen: Thank you, Uncle Josh, for telling us the rest of what happened and someday we will go on this quest but for right now, our place is here with you.

Archer: That is right uncle, if you don't mind us sticking around a little longer.

Josh: Mind, of course I don't mind and when the time comes for you to go. I will be okay, as long as you come back to see me. One night as their uncle was returning from selling some bows and arrows to one of the shops, he was attacked, robbed, and killed in one of the alleys. Losing their uncle was painful, but they had learned over the years to control their anger. They also knew that their uncle would not have wanted them to go out and harm someone just because of him.

2: The Quest

Now they were on their own, so they decided to sell the shop and everything in it; because they were going to do some traveling and find out what this quest was all about. They were going to try their luck, at some of the bow tournaments across this country, to make money to live on and it would let them see more of this country, which they had been living in and now called home. The boys had both grown into handsome young men. Bowen was six feet tall, husky built with lots of muscles from years of hard work. He had blonde hair and dark bright blue eyes. Archer was well built from working hard too. He was six feet and two inches tall with jet black hair and big brown eyes. This country was different than anything they had ever seen. Hurricane Island from what little they could remember was ocean, sand, a few mountains with very little grass and a lot of coconut trees. This country had mountains, sandy beaches, stone roads, and a lot of grassy fields, many different kinds of trees and a lot of buildings. When they left the coast, they began to see other parts of the country where they had dirt roads, a lot of grass, a lot of trees, some small ponds here and there and a lot of animals. The trees were different too. These trees were shorter, instead of a few large leaves; they had lots of little leaves. Some of them made perfect shade trees. There were also trees that had fruit that could be eaten.

They entered the first town that they came to after selling the shop and leaving the ocean's shore, which they had called home for over thirteen years. The streets were dirt instead of stone. The buildings were a little farther apart and weren't as tall. The first man they ran into told them that the wizard, who lived behind the stable wanted to talk to them.

Bowen: How do you know that it is us, he wants to talk to?

The man: (He laughed!) I was told to tell the first man, that I saw with a crazy looking bow, to come see him. Your bow sure is crazy looking to me!

Archer: (He laughed.) He has you there, that bow is strange looking all right. They walked down the street and turned into the alley which led behind the stable. Before they could knock on the door, a voice from inside called out: Come on in, the door is not locked. It was a dusty room with a dirt floor and one long wooden bench against one of the walls where the man slept. There was a round table, in the middle of the room, with four bales of hay for seats. The man was seated on one of them when they entered the room.

Merlin: Hi, my name is Merlin. Please sit down. The boys were both curious, wanting to know what he had to say, so they sat down and listened.

Bowen: So, you wanted to see us?

Merlin: Yes! You have made a special bow and your brother there, has made some special arrows to go with it. They are both magical items. The special bow and arrows that you have made are weapons, for the one special person who will save this country from being destroyed. They sat quietly listening, as Merlin told them about things, that they had done. The things that he told them about were things that they had done in their past and there was no way that he should have known about them. He also told them about the Chosen One. He told them, that they both could use the bow or the arrows, but neither of them, could use them together. The only one, who will be able to use them both together, is the Chosen One. These magical items are the weapons which are needed to keep the people of this land from being destroyed. You must find the person who can use both of them together and give them to that person. You must also help that person in any way that you can.

Archer: How will we know who the Chosen One is? What is his name? What does he look like?

Merlin: I don't know the answer to those questions. All I can tell you is that person will be able to use your special bow and his special arrows together. That is all the help that I can give you. You must give them to the Chosen

One! Give them to the one who can use them together. Our very lives depend on it!

Bowen: Any suggestions as to where, to start looking for this person?

Merlin: The bow tournaments. Any bowman worth his salt will be competing at them. I can tell you no more, so leave me. Just leave me!

The boys got up and left Merlin walking back toward the front of the stable. Bowen: He was a strange man. How did he know all of that stuff about us?

Archer: I don't know. How did he know about the bow and arrows? Also, he basically told us the same thing our parents did about them, except he talked more about the person we have to give them to.

Bowen: Yeah, he kept calling the person, the Chosen One and how they were going to save this country.

They spent the night in the stable and slept in the hay loft, after cleaning out the stalls as payment, so the owner would let them stay. Early the next morning they left town, traveling toward the town of Oakville and the first tournament. Bowen and Archer were evenly matched, when it came to using Bowen's special bow. The winner of the tournament would always be one of them. No one else in the tournament even came close to shooting as well. The boy's skills were not limited just to bow shooting. They were equally as good with swords, spears, and other weapons. Even though they were just as good with the other weapons, they liked the bow and arrows the best.

Other men, who had shot against them in the tournament, would try and buy the bow, thinking that was why they could shoot that good, but the bow was not for sale. The boys would let them try and shoot it, just to rule them out as being the Chosen One. When they could not shoot it, then they were no longer interested in buying it. A visiting King from another country once ordered them, to sell him the bow.

Bowen: Your Royal Highness, the bow is not for sale, but we would gladly give the bow to you as a gift, if you can shoot it. You know that if you cannot shoot it, then the bow is no good to you and in that case, we would keep it. The King agreed to their offer. He tried to shoot the bow but could not. He let the boys keep the bow and they were on their way again.

The boys had been on the road going from one tournament to another looking for the Chosen One. They had built up a nice little nest egg along the way. The next tournament was in the town of Plum Orchard. When they arrived in town, they started looking for a place to spend the night. They were passing an alley, when they saw a young man, who looked to be a few years younger than them. Two men were following the lad. They were getting ready to rob him and one of them had already pulled out a knife. Archer and Bowen decided to help the boy out. They each moved out of sight, on each side of the alley and waited for the boy to pass, where they were hidden. After he had passed where they were hidden, Bowen and Archer stepped out with their swords drawn. Bowen: Hey! Can we help the two of you? The second man had already pulled his knife out too, before he saw the boys. Both men stopped and told them that they did not want any trouble, as both of the men put their knives back into the cases that hung on their belts. The two men turned around and quickly went the other direction. They heard a voice coming from behind them.

The Boy: You will regret helping me, but I am thankful for the help. We better get out of here, before they come back with their friends. Archer and Bowen turned around and faced the boy. The boy: Hi! My name is James. James was nineteen years old, six feet tall with a thin lanky toned body and hazel eyes. His hair was brown with a streak of gray, which looked like a lightning bolt.

James: Thank you again for the help. Come, go with me, those men will be back with their friends and trust me; you don't want to be here, when they do return.

The boys were right about him being younger than they were for Bowen and Archer were now twenty-four years old. Archer: Hi! My name is Archer, and this is my brother Bowen. They followed James out of the alley, down the street and into an herb shop, which sold magical herbs and potions. James locked the shop door behind them. He then led them through the shop into the back and up a set of narrow stairs into the attic of the building. The attic was a small room, with four long benches along the walls. There was a small table and only one chair.

James: Make yourself at home! You can spend the night here, if you want to. I will be leaving early in the morning to go to the tournament in the next town.

Archer: That is where we are going too. Do you mind if we travel with you?

Bowen: We are going to enter and compete in the bow shooting contest.

James: Sure, that would be great. There is safety in numbers and it will be good to have some help if we run into those men again tomorrow. Each boy stretched out on one of the long wooden benches and went to sleep.

James woke them up early the next morning.

Wake up! We have to leave before the master returns or I will never get to leave this place.

Bowen: Master! Are you a slave?

James: (He laughed.) Slave, no. I am the master wizard's apprentice. That is something which I no longer want to be. I know that if I am still here when he returns, he will not let me leave; even if he has to use magic to keep me here. Apprentice, now that is a joke. He never taught me any real magic, just tricks like vanishing in a cloud of smoke. He worked me like a slave. Clean this, dust that, and bring me whatever. The boys quickly gathered their things and they all three left the shop together. Archer started laughing as they walked down the street.

James: What is so funny?

Archer: James, now that you don't have a master wizard over you anymore, I guess that makes you the master wizard. James stood thinking about it for a minute then he laughed and continued walking.

James: I guess you are right. Master wizard, I like the sound of that, it sounds really good to me.

The tournament started in about an hour, so as soon as they arrived in town, Bowen and Archer signed up for the bow shooting contest.

There weren't as many events at this tournament. The swordsmen were still recovering from the last tournament. They had jesters and jugglers entertaining the crowd while they waited for each of the events to be set up and to start. The first event this time was stone throwing instead of the knife throwing in the last tournament. The contestants would all throw the same medium size stone. The ten who threw it the farthest, went on to the next round. For the next round, they would throw a little larger size stone. The five that threw it the farthest, went on to the next round. For the last round, they would throw an extra-large stone. The one that threw it the farthest would be the winner.

Bowen and Archer wondered if any of these muscle-bound men could be the Chosen One. They would try to get them to try to pull back the special bow with the special arrows, to see if they could even draw it back and shoot it. They would tell them it was another strength test, and they could win the bow and arrows. That should be enough, to get them to try, but it would have to wait. The bow shooting event, which was the second event, was starting. They got to the one-hundred-yard target again. This tournament was different. There was a tall skinny boy, who hid his identity, shooting against them. This boy was matching Archer and Bowen, shot for shot.

Bowen: Archer do you think that we might

have found the one which we have been searching for?

Archer: Let's find out! Boy, I will give you this fine bow and arrows, if you can use them together and hit the center of the target, but you have to use these arrows in this bow. The boy did not say a word but reached for the bow and arrows.

A guard grabbed the boy before he could take the special bow and arrows from Archer. The guard then removed the boy's hood, to reveal a five foot four-inch-tall tomboy, with a well-built body for her age of nineteen years. She had dimples at the top of her cheeks and freckles across her nose. The girl had long blond hair, which she had twisted up on top of her head to hide it, and large blue eyes. Guard: You know that women are not allowed to shoot or compete in these contests. A woman's place is in the home, cooking and cleaning. Now off with you before I have to tell your father what you have been up to. She smiled at the boys then left.

Bowen: What a shame. She was such a good shot.

Archer: I agree, and she was not bad looking either. They both laughed.

James had been watching them, from the stands. He wondered about the strange bow and arrows that the boys carried. It reminded him of part of the Legend, which he had read and wondered if the Legend was true. During the times, when the wizard had left him, and he was by himself, James had read several of the wizard's books. There had been two Legends in the book. One was about a great King who had pulled a special sword out of a stone. The other Legend was about a Chosen One, who had a special bow and arrows that paved the way for the other to become King. At the time, they sounded like interesting stories, but he thought it would be more important that he copy the spells out of Merlin's spell book, so he could learn them. He remembered the description of the bow and arrows from the Chosen One's Legend. He thought that the ones the boys had could be the same ones from the Legend.

As James was trying to remember more of the legend, some other memories came back to him. He remembered how strict but protective the wizard was of him as he was growing up. He had been with the wizard as long as he could remember. To start with, the wizard would read him stories. His favorite one to read to James was the Legend of the great King. He knew that one very well. But the one he needed to remember now was the one about the Chosen One. The wizard had been kind to him. He also did magic tricks to entertain him when he was younger, which made him later love the idea of being his apprentice. As he got older,

Merlin only taught him little tricks with cards and hiding a nut under a cup, they were just sleight of hand tricks, not real magic. Whenever, James would ask him to show him some real magic, he refused saying James was not mature enough or responsible enough to learn real magic yet. The wizard would just keep giving James more and more chores for him to do to keep him busy. Merlin told him that it would teach him responsibility. Once he taught him how to disappear in a cloud of smoke, but it was just another trick, not real magic.

James decided if he was ever going to learn some real magic that he would have to teach himself. So, when the wizard was away he would read his magic book. He tried to do some of the spells, but the wizard caught him and gave him even more chores. James was feeling more and more like a slave, than a wizard's apprentice. So, on the rare occasions, when he was left alone, he would copy down as many of the spells as he could until he had copied down all of the spells that were in the wizard's book. In between copying the spells down, he would practice first one and then another of the spells that seemed easier. It took him a while to master even a few of them, because it took him some time to figure out that pronunciation and rhythm was crucial to cast a spell. He didn't have any problem with rhythm, but he did have a problem with his pronunciation. James had to figure a way out of his situation. The wizard kept him too busy to learn very much on his own and he was tired of feeling like a slave.

It was just luck that he had run into Bowen and Archer when he did. He was so glad to be away from the slave driving wizard. He sat there trying to remember what the Legend had said and now he wished that he had written it down too. While he was trying to remember the legend, his thoughts were interrupted. When the guard grabbed the boy, who turned out to be a girl brought him back to the present. She had been matching Bowen and Archer shot for shot. If that wasn't impressive, he didn't know what was. Besides she was also very beautiful. James had never seen anyone like her before; she shot like a man but looked like an angel. Since they took the girl out, it only left Bowen and Archer to shoot.

Bowen won the tournament that time, by splitting Archer's last arrow when he shot. James met them after they were done shooting and had collected their prize money. While the third event was going on, which was the jousting competition, the three of them went to talk to the muscle men. It wasn't hard to get them to try and the more that tried, the more the others wanted to try also, none of the muscle men was the Chosen One either. They allowed the bowmen that hadn't tried before try their luck, again none of them could draw the bow back either. They didn't wait for the tournament to be over. Bowen had already collected his winnings, so they started their long walk toward the town of Carnesville and the next tournament.

About halfway to the next town, they stopped and made camp for the night. Bowen: James did you know the girl they took out of the bow shooting contest, at the last tournament?

James: Only by reputation of being the best bow shooter anywhere. At least until you two showed up. I also heard she was pretty, but that was an understatement.

Bowen and Archer agreed that James was right about that last part when they heard horses approaching. James had gone into the woods and hid! Bowen and Archer remained by their campfire and waited. They were both ready to fight if they had to. Two of the King's guards rode up and dismounted. Guard: Have you seen anyone?

Bowen: I have not seen anyone since we left the tournament.

Guard: We are looking for the King's daughter and the wizard's apprentice.

Bowen: I don't believe I have ever seen the King's daughter, but I did see the wizard's apprentice at the tournament.

Guard: Are you not the one who won the tournament?

Bowen: Yes, I won it. Why?

Guard: Then you did see the King's daughter. She was the one, who was about to beat you, before they made her quit shooting.

Archer: Oh! So that is who she was! That is the last time we saw her. Is she in trouble?

Guard: No! I am sure that she has just run away again. She is always running away. If you see them, let us know!

Bowen: How about the apprentice of the wizard, what is he wanted for? The guards mounted their horses.

Guard: The wizard has always told us where she is hiding so we can find her. He refused to help us this time unless we find his apprentice and return him. The poor fellow! The wizard used him like a slave; we don't really blame him for leaving, but we have no choice. If we find him, we will have to take him back to the wizard. The guards rode away.

3: Master Wizard

James walks into camp with the girl behind him and her sword in his back. James: Stop poking me with that sword! I was not going to tell them where you were. They are looking for me too. I don't want to go back any more than you do.

Bowen: The guards are gone now. Do you think that you could take your sword out of our friend's back? (She lowered her sword.) My name is Bowen and that is my brother Archer. The one who's back you were poking; his name is James. He was the wizard's apprentice, which the guards were also looking for. What is your name, or should we just call you princess?

She pointed her sword toward Bowen: My name is Kieris and don't you forget it!

Archer: Welcome! He pointed toward a tree stump. Have a seat near the fire; it is getting a little chilly out here. Kieris sat down on the stump.

Kieris: Well, how about that offer? Does it still stand or are you against women shooting too?

Archer: What offer?

Bowen: Of course the offer is still good. Shoot my strange looking bow, with one of Archer's

strange looking arrows, hit the center of the target and you get to own them both.
Archer: Bowen!

Bowen: The Legend does not say male or female!

Archer: You are right! The offer stands!

Kieris: Good, then set up your target. She picked up her bow and one of the special arrows, shot and hit the target dead center. I just wanted to make sure, that these were not some kind of trick arrows or a trick bow, before I tried to win them. She then picked up Bowen's bow and put one of her arrows in it and again hit the target dead center. Archer and Bowen looked at each other, they were both surprised, and up until then, they had been the only ones, who could even shoot the bow. They were the only ones, who could shoot the special arrows and hit anything. The boys held their breaths as she got ready to shoot. Had they found the true owner of the bow and its arrows? She put one of the special arrows, in the special bow and lined it up for her shot. With the special arrow and the bow together, she could not even pull the bow string back, to shoot it. She took the arrow and put it into her bow and shot it without any problem. Kieris: I don't understand. She handed Bowen back the bow. Here you shoot it with those crazy arrows.

Bowen: I can't shoot them together either. No one can. They are magical and only the Chosen One, which the Legend talks about, will be able to use them together.

Archer: We know this because Merlin told us, that only the Chosen One would be able to shoot it. But I will give you this, until now Bowen and I were the only ones who could shoot the bow with regular arrows and hit anything.

Bowen: Or a regular bow, with one of the crooked arrows and hit the target.

James had been quietly watching and listening. James: Do any of you know what the Legend says? They all shook their heads no. James: Well, I don't remember it all, but what I do remember reading, was that a band of friends, from different places, will save the Chosen One's friend. That will make them friends and together bring the Chosen One, into their full power. Since you two hold the Chosen One's bow and arrows, I guess that makes us the band of friends.

Bowen: How many members, does the band have?

James: I don't know, but so far, I am the only one, that you have saved. I can't be the Chosen One's friend, because I don't have any friends.

Bowen: You mean that you did not have any friends.

Archer: That is right! For now, we are your friends.

Kieris: You are part of this band of friends and we are hunting for the Chosen One. So that makes us all friends, just like the Legend said. James! Have you tried to shoot the bow?

James: Who me? I have never shot a bow or anything in my life!

Archer: I see what you are thinking! James, go ahead and at least try. James took the special bow and one of Bowen's regular arrows and made a perfect shot.

Bowen: Wow! Bowen handed him another bow and one of the special arrows. Again, he made a perfect shot. Kieris handed him a plain arrow, to go with the plain bow. This time, he could not hit anything.

James: I don't understand!

Kieris: It is simple, whoever can shoot the bow or one of the special arrows and hits the target, is part of this band of friends. If they can't, then they cannot join us.

James: I see, a friend's test!

Kieris: So, what else do you know how to do, master wizard? She smiled at him and he smiled back.

James: Master Wizard, I do like the sound of that, when you say it. I wish I was a master wizard! The only things the wizard ever taught we were tricks, sleight of hand, misdirection but no real magic. What magic I know, I learned on my own from his book. I even mastered a few that would help me with my cleaning and chores, so it would make it easier and faster that way and would give me more time to practice. James began to laugh.

Kieris: What's so funny?

James: With the magic I have learned, I would make someone an excellent homemaker. All four of them burst out laughing at that.

Kieris: All it takes is practice, practice, and more practice.

James: Will you help me? You know, make sure that I am pronouncing the words right. I have the rhythm of how the words are supposed to be said, but my pronunciation needs a lot of work.

Kieris: Sure! I think that the first spell, you should try to learn should be anything that will help protect us.

James: Sure! Here is my book of spells, you pick out the ones that you think that I should learn first. He handed her a very large book, which he had copied all the wizard's spells into. She took the book, sat down on the stump near the fire, and started looking through it.

Kieris: This one might be a good one to start with if it works like I think it will. We can practice it anytime you want to.

James: What do you think that this spell will do? He took the book and looked at the spell, which she had picked out.

Kieris: Here read this one, cast it on that squirrel over there and let's see how it works.

James: He looked at the squirrel and started to read aloud from the book. He filled in the blanks to make it work on the squirrel. (Squirrel, I see you in truth and light and this way remain in my sight. From others fade and hide from their sight. All, others will see when they look at you, is a big fat frog. Kieris looked at the squirrel but all she saw was a frog.
Kieris: James is the squirrel still there?

James: Yes!

Kieris: You did it! What I see there is a big fat frog. It worked! Now practice on other things and all you have to do is ask me what I see to know if the spell worked or not. You need to practice, until you can hide what or rather who we are, when others look at us. I think it would be a good idea to only work on one spell at a time. Master this spell then I will pick out another one for you.

James: Ok! Master one spell at a time. That sounds good, I will do whatever you say. They all went to bed for the night.

Early the next morning as they were breaking camp, they heard the guard's horses; they were returning. James hid in the woods and fearing for the princess, tried to cast the spell on her. Princess to me is seen in truth and light, but from others hide her from their sight. When others look at her, be friend or foe, all they will see is a tall thin boy where she should be. The guards dismounted and walked over to the boys. The princess was still covered up and asleep. They had let her sleep in, until it was time to leave. One of the guards gently kicked the blanket she was under, to wake whoever was there.

Guard: Get up! I want to see, who you are! He reached down and pulled the blanket off the princess. Bowen and Archer stood up, ready to draw their swords and defend her, if they had to.

Guard: Don't you ever feed this boy? He is nothing but a rack of bones. Bowen and Archer were both surprised to see a boy where the princess should have been, but they did not say anything. James walked out of the woods, after putting ashes on the gray lightning bolt in his hair to hide it. He was willing to give himself up to protect her.

James: You will have to excuse my brother, he does not talk, an accident when he was born.

Guard: You look something like the wizard's apprentice, but you can't be. He was an only child and did not have any brothers and sisters. You don't have the gray lightning bolt in your hair, which the wizard put there to mark you. Sorry lad that I woke you! He turned to the other guard: I don't know what to do now! If we go back without the princess, the King will have us beheaded. Kieris felt bad for the guards, because she had no doubt that the King would behead them if the mood struck him, but she could not think of that now, going back would only help them for a little while and would surely condemn her. No, she couldn't go back; she had to stay and help them find the Chosen One, so they could help the Chosen One save them all. The guards got on their horses and left.

Bowen turned back to the boy: Who are you?

Kieris: I told you that my name was Kieris, have you forgotten already? She laughed. She knew what the wizard had done.

Kieris: Good job, James! It was Kieris' voice coming from this boy.

James: (He laughed!) Make Bowen and Archer be able to see Kieris, in truth and light, but keep her a boy, in everyone else's sight. Now Bowen and Archer could see her.

Bowen: Good trick, master wizard! (He patted James on the back.) James looked at Kieris and smiled: Now, that was real magic, thanks to Kieris. She picked out the perfect spell at the right time for me to learn. James laughed.

Kieris: Now what is so funny? James walked over and put his hand on her shoulder.

James: I guess I will have to find a new name for you, little brother. (They all laughed.)

Kieris: I guess I will have to practice talking with a deeper voice.

4: World Tournament

They packed up the camp and moved on toward the next town and tournament. James stayed out of sight to keep anyone from spotting him. Kieris went and signed up for the bow shooting event; they also found out what events would be held and in what order at this tournament. The only entertainment this time were the bards walking around singing their stories of great battles, strength, and skill from earlier tournaments. They even heard one of the bards singing about Bowen and Archer. How the brothers with such great skill and deadly aim could not be defeated by anyone but each other. The first event was sword fighting. Kieris understood that you had to practice to be good and even put on demonstrations to show off your skills; but these men were trying to kill each other just to prove who was best. It was so barbaric, that she could not watch the senseless gore, so they all took a walk. They went and checked out the merchants stands. There was a stand for anything and everything that you could think of. Each thing had its own stand; there was a different stand for each kind of weapon, each piece of armor, men's clothes, women's clothes, jewelry for men and women, cooked foods, horses, dry goods, cattle, fruits, vegetables, tools for different trades, musical instruments and the list goes on and on.

The second event was knife throwing, which

none of them was interested in watching. They decided to get something to eat while they waited, so they went back to the different food stands. They didn't feel like cooking, and didn't really have the time; so they checked out the fruit stand and the stands that had cooked food. There were several meats to choose from; rabbit, fish, squirrel, chicken, beef, and pork. Then there were a few cooked vegetables to choose from; roasted potatoes, corn on the cob, mashed potatoes, green beans, and pinto beans. There were even hot fresh breads to choose from; white or wheat loaf bread, white or wheat rolls and corn bread. Bowen decided on the rabbit, mashed potatoes with gravy and wheat roll to go with his apple he had gotten from the fruit stand. Archer got squirrel, green beans, and a white roll to go with his pear. James got pork, corn on the cob and a white roll to go with his peach. Kieris got beef, mashed potatoes with extra gravy and a loaf of white bread to go with her strawberries. After they all had their food and had gotten some water to drink, they went away from everyone else and sat under a shade tree to eat, so they would not be disturbed.

They made sure that they stayed in hearing distance of the bards, so they would know what event was taking place. The third event was staff fighting; none of them had ever seen a competition like that and didn't want to miss it. They talked a little about the different events while they ate. They had just finished eating when they heard the bards singing how happy they were that the second event was over. They all got up, threw their trash away and headed back toward the arena. They were lucky to find enough seats, so they could sit together. It seemed like everyone wanted to watch this competition. Like the sword fights, when you were defeated in battle, then you were eliminated, but this was a more civilized battle. To be defeated you had to be on the ground and couldn't get up, surrender, or be disarmed. A few of the contestants wore armor but most of them did not. The ones with the armor were eliminated quickly, because they couldn't move as fast and the armor made it too difficult to get back up, once they were knocked down.

Most of the contestants had good sportsmanship; as once their opponent was down or disarmed, they didn't take cheap shots at them. They all liked this event much better than the first one. Some of contestants also had some real skills a few even did moves and used techniques none of them had ever seen before. There were two more events before theirs. The forth event was stone throwing, which would not last long. There were only a few muscle men that entered. When the contestants were called to line up, everyone either laughed or was yelling at a couple of the contestants. The boys just shook their heads and smiled, because they came from an ocean port, so they had already seen men like these, while Kieris turned her head and made noises like she was going to throw up. They could not help themselves and laughed at her reaction to the sight of these men.

Both contestants were from the Orient, like the other contestants, they were not wearing any shirts, but instead of seeing muscles, you saw an extra-large round belly. They also were not wearing pants but had on, what looked like a big thick sheet tied under their huge bellies and barely covering their butts. The announcer raised his hands for silence: If I may have your attention. These men are our guest in this country, please do not yell or laugh at them, for in their country this is one of the ways they dress to do battle. Later two men, also from this country will be putting on a demonstration, of one of their events, that is held in their country. They will have even less on for the demonstration, so ladies please, be prepared to turn your heads or have your fans handy, to cover your faces, during this event.

Everyone calmed down and the event began. The boys checked on Kieris to see if she was okay. She said that she was okay and that she was glad they would not be around for the demonstration, because she didn't want to see them with less on, as she made a weird face. Bowen and Archer could not help but laugh again. She gave them both a dirty look and then asked them to tell her when the event was over, as she turned her head away from the field again. With only a few contestants, it didn't last long, one of the oriental men won.

The fifth event was spear throwing; it was another event Bowen, Archer and Kieris had not seen, so they were interested in watching this event. The announcer explained the rules: There will only be three targets for this event. The first is a large target painted on the ground. Each contestant will be given a different white scarf with a different number on it, to put on their spears, and then each one will throw their spears trying to hit the bull's eye. The spears will stay on the field until everyone has thrown. The one closest to the center of the bull's eye will get fifty points plus one point for each person who didn't hit the bull's eye. Everyone else who hits the bull's eye will get twenty-five points plus one point for each person who didn't hit the bull's eye. Everyone who hits the ring around the bull's eye will get ten points plus one point for each person who didn't make it that close to the bull's eye plus the person in that ring closest to the bull's eye gets an extra five points.

Everyone who hits the second ring from the bull's eye gets five points plus one point for each person who didn't make it that close to the bull's eye plus the person in that ring closest to the bull's eye gets an extra five points. Anyone outside those rings will get no points. It doesn't matter if it is thrown off to one side or the other, short, or over thrown.

Points will be awarded according to position and distance from the center of the bull's eye. Any spears that don't stick in the ground will get no points. Before each target I will be explaining the point system to everyone. The person with the most points, after all three targets is the winner. If there is a tie, those contestants will throw for distance, the farthest one will be the winner. If there is a tie there, they will throw until one is farther than the other. Again, if the spear doesn't stick in the ground at this point then that person will be eliminated.

The center of the bull's eye for this target was exactly 30 yards from the throw line, but the contestants were not told this, for this target was to test accuracy and being able to judge distance, that is why the points were so high. This round also took a while, even though there were only fifteen contestants, because of all the measuring that needed to be done. The second target was scored the same as the first, but it was a big round wooden wheel with a target painted on it and it was standing upright 35 yards away, as before they didn't tell them the distance. This round didn't take as long to score, because half of them didn't even hit the target and a couple were knocked out of the target so they didn't count either. The third target was an old suit of armor filled with straw and a heart painted on it where the heart would be on a person. It was a moving target this time, so each contestant would throw and if the spear made a hole in the armor, whether it fell out or not, that hole counted and was marked by that contestant's number that was given to them at the start of the event. The armor was mounted on a platform with wheels and a rope on either side of it, so it could be pulled from a distance across the field.

If the contestants hit a hand or foot, they got one point. If the hit was in the arm or leg, they got five points. If the hit was in the gut, they got ten points. If the hit was in the head or chest, they got fifteen points. If hit was in the heart, they got fifty points. If no one hit the heart, then the one who hit the chest and was the closest to the heart got an extra ten points. Only five hit the target; one in the leg, one in the gut, one in the head and two in the chest, but no one hit the heart, so they had to measure. While the three judges were adding up the scores and checking them, Kieris was starting to get excited; because the next event was the bow shooting, and this would be the first competition, which she would get to finish.

They finally announced the winner of the fifth event and called for all the contestants for the sixth event, which was bow shooting, to gather around. They had added some new targets and wanted to explain the additional rules for these targets. As before, they had the twenty, thirty and fifty-yard targets, they took away the one-hundred-yard target because no one usually made it that far, they added three other targets. These targets would test the contestant's skills more than the old ones, because they were moving targets. This time, you still had to hit the bull's eye of the stationary targets to move on, the moving targets were the top half of the shooters that hit the target, or if you hit the bull's eye on these targets guaranteed moving on to the next round. Anyone that was left at the last target, if it was two or twelve, would all shoot at the same target.

Bowen, Archer and Kieris all looked at each other and smiled because they knew that this was going to be fun. They drew straws between themselves to see which one of the three would shoot last. Kieris was smiling; she had already decided to use her own bow to shoot; now they would see what kind of skills she had. When she drew the short straw and knew she would shoot last, then she laughed. The boys asked her what was funny, but all she would say is that they would see. There were forty-five contestants that signed up for this event. They each took turns shooting at the twenty-yard target that stood still. They all hit the target but only thirty of them hit the bull's eye, since they did all thirty got to go on to the next round. This round had eliminated fifteen. The second target was a moving one; they would roll a medium sized wooden wheel with a target painted on it across the field to be shot at the twenty-five-yard mark. Out of the thirty contestants, ten missed the target, twenty hit the target but only ten hit the bull's eye. This time there was less than half that hit the bull's eye, so the five closest to the bull's eye and the ten that hit the bull's eye got to go on to the next round.

The third target was at the thirty-yard mark and stood still. Out of the fifteen contestants in this round, all of them hit the target, but only twelve hit the bull's eye. All twelve that did move on to the next round. The forth target was a smaller round wheel with a target painted on it. At the forty-yard mark it would be put in a sling and shot straight up in the air. Out of the twelve contestants in this round, nine of them hit the target, but only eight of the nine had hit the bull's eye. All eight that hit the bull's eye were moving on to the next round. Bowen, Archer and Kieris all noticed before that this was one of the largest yearly tournaments, so there was a lot more competing. They knew that a lot of them had traveled a long distance, even some from other countries, just to shoot in this tournament. Of course, they would not travel that far, if they didn't think they could honestly win, so now they were noticing how much better the bowman were. It didn't worry Bowen and Archer at all, but since Kieris was shooting with her own bow, it was starting to put a little more pressure on her, but she was still determined to show them all how good she was.

There were eight of them to shoot at the fifth target; it was at the fifty-yard mark standing still. All eight of the contestants hit the target but only five hit the bull's eye, so five of them would move on to the last round and sixth target. The announcer asked for everyone to get quiet, and then he explained that it was important, that everyone be completely quiet, while the bowman shot at the last target, because it would take a lot of skill and concentration to hit it. The sixth and last target was at the sixty-yard mark and it was a moving target. It was another even smaller round wheel with a target painted on it. The target was hanging from a branch of a dead tree, so nothing was shading it and was swinging back and forth like a pendulum. Everyone got silent when the first bowman stepped up to shoot, he barely hit the target. Bowen was next and of course he hit the bull's eye. Even though they were told to be quiet everyone cheered. Once that they were silent again the third bowman stepped up. He missed the target completely, but hit the center of the trunk, of the tree right behind the target.

Bowen, Archer and Kieris looked at each other and were thinking the same thing. If the bowman had timed it a little better, he could not only have hit the target but maybe the bull's eye. Could this bowman be the Chosen

One? They would have to make sure he got to try the special bow and arrows. It was now Archer's turn, as usual Archer split Bowen's shaft and buried his arrow inside Bowen's arrow. Again, the crowd could not control themselves and cheer again. While they were waiting, for them to quiet down again, Bowen asked Kieris, if she wanted to borrow, his bow for her last shot. Kieris smiled: No. After shooting the whole match with my bow, I would rather finish with it. Besides if I miss, we still don't loose and after the other man coming so close, I want to see if I can do better than him. Bowen understood and shook his head yes.

The crowd got quiet and Kieris was next. She stepped up to shoot and you could hear mumbling from the crowd. As far as they were concerned it was over, because they were already surprised that this skinny boy had lasted this long. It made her mad, they were still judging her on how she looked and not her skills. She took a deep breath and let it out slowly to calm her nerves, then tuned out the noise the crowd was making and took her shot. It split Archer's shaft and buried her arrow inside his arrow. Everyone's mouth dropped open, even Bowen and Archer and then the whole crowd went to hooping, yelling, and cheering. No one there had ever seen two arrows split before. It was the first tournament that she had been allowed to finish, because they could not see that she was a girl and she didn't have to worry about the King's guards stopping her or the King finding out.

The King's men were also present at the tournament; they were looking for the princess and the apprentice. James had stayed hidden, just in case one of the guards knew him, from before. He was so proud of Kieris that he almost gave his hiding place away, when a guard walked by near him. He couldn't wait to congratulate her; what he really wanted to do is take her in his arms and show her how much he cared for her. But he figured she would probably fall in love, with either Bowen or Archer and he would not stand a chance. Just for starters, they were both older, better looking than he was and because they shared the same passion with her, the love of bow shooting.

While the seventh and last event was going on, which was jousting, Bowen and Archer were letting the bowmen and muscle men try the special bow and arrows. Kieris had gone to collect her prize money. She wasn't gone long, until she was back, and you could tell she was a little upset. Archer walked over to her to see what was wrong, while Bowen continued to let the men try to shoot the bow, but Bowen kept glancing over to see if it was something that they needed him for. Archer: What is wrong, you seem upset? Kieris: We have to wait until the end of the tournament before they will give me my money. They said that they had scheduled an awards ceremony to present the money and prizes to the winners. Archer looked at Bowen and motioned that everything was okay.

Archer looked back at Kieris and smiled: So, we will just spend the night in town, why would that upset you? Kieris: I was hoping to be able to leave and find a good campsite and avoid having to be in town to long. Too many things could go wrong. I am disguised but James isn't, and I don't want anything to happen to him. (She blushed.) I mean I would hate for anything to happen to him just because we have to stick around for me to collect my winnings. Archer laughed: I understand, but we will be fine. Having this many people around will allow us to sneak him into the inn easier, as long as we don't do anything to attract attention to ourselves. Bowen was finished letting everyone try to shot the bow, so he then walked over to where Kieris and Archer were standing. Bowen: So, what is going on? Archer explained about them needing to spend the night at the inn and why. Except he left out Kieris being overly concerned for James, he would tell Bowen about that later. Bowen looked at Kieris: It would be nice to sleep in a bed and it shouldn't be any problem to sneak James into the inn. Kieris: The other thing is the demonstration is right before the awards ceremony and I really didn't want to be here for that. She made a disgusted face that made Bowen and Archer laugh. She gave both of them a look that said she wanted to smack them. Kieris: Since there is no way out around staying, I will defiantly need a good bath if I have to see those nasty men again. This time all three of them laughed.

From James' hiding place he could see all three of them most of the time but kept a close eye on Kieris in case she needed him. When he saw her walking back to where Archer and Bowen was, she looked so upset that he almost came out of hiding, but two guards had walked over and were now standing next to his hiding place. It was breaking his heart that she was upset, and he could not help her. As he watched, he saw how Archer helped calm her down and then Bowen got her to laugh. Oh, how he loved the sound of her laugh. A thought crossed his mind, which made him sadder. This is another good reason for her to choose one of them instead of him. The jousting was over and so Bowen and Archer found a seat, while Kieris gathered with the other contestants that won their events. Kieris was relieved that the guys weren't with her to make fun of her reactions to the demon-stration. Announcer: If I may have your attention. The demonstration will start in a minute, again I would ask that you don't laugh or yell at our guest. They have come a long way to put on this exhibition of Sumo Wrestling. Ladies have your fans ready to cover your face or look away. Parents, you may want to have your children look away during this also.

Two oriental men walked out, there was some snickering, but no one laughed out loud. You could hear some of the ladies gasping at what they saw and parents telling their children to look away, so the kids would not laugh at the men. Just like the oriental men from the forth event, they wore no shirt but this time instead of a thick sheet tied just below their huge bellies, they had taken the heavy thick sheets and fixed them, so they would be completely out of the way, so they could use their legs better. This time Bowen and Archer were even surprised at the way they were dressed. They had seen the thick sheet before but not this. The thick sheets were folded, and they wore them like diapers that covered their whole bottoms. Everyone in the crowd had a hard time trying not to laugh at grown men in diapers.

5: The Trap

After waiting a few minutes for everyone to settle down, the speaker put up his hands to get everyone's attention and waited for them to get quiet. Announcer: This is a Sumo Wrestling Exhibition, in this event; the two wrestlers will show their skills of how this is done. There is NO punching or kicking allowed. They have to get their opponents down, which is easier said than done. Begin! They began by raising one leg, stomping it down and putting their hand on that knee; then they raised the other leg, stomped it down and put their hand on that knee. All at once, they both went charging at each other like a bull. They ran into each other, using their speed and all of their weight to try to knock each other down with their bellies. When that didn't work, they tried shoving each other down. They repeated the same two things again, charge and then shove. Finally, they grabbed each other's arms, tried to hook their leg behind the other ones leg and then tried to use their weight to get the other one down. The announcer was right these big men were like mountains, hard to move and even harder to put down, even though they were about the same size. It took just a little while longer, but one finally got the other one down. The crowd cheered, Kieris didn't know if they were cheering because it was over or because they liked the demonstration, even though see didn't watch, she was glad it was over.

Now it was time for the awards ceremony. They had the winners of each event line up in the same order as the events they won.

Announcer: Now for the awards to our winners, they will be receiving the cash purse for each event that was already posted plus this year, we decided to award them other prizes also. Please wait until the winner has actually received their cash and prizes before you cheer for them, that way you don't miss any of the prizes. I will be calling the winners up in the same order as the events were held, so please be patient and don't yell out who you want called next. Thank you.

The first event was Sword Fighting; the winner of that event was Tommy of England. The crowd cheered as Tommy walked out onto the stage. The announcer waited until they calmed down. Announcer: If you don't wait until I tell you what they won and give the prizes to them, then we will not continue, and you will not know what all they have won. (The crowd got quiet.) Tommy, I present to you, the cash purse for your event and a top of the line new suit of armor with everything that goes with it. Tommy took the cash purse and his prizes. The crowd hesitated and then began to cheer. When Tommy left the stage and the crowd calmed down, he began again: The second event was Knife Throwing; the winner of that event was Denver of Scotland. Denver walked out onto the stage, but the crowd was silent. Announcer smiled: Denver, I present to you, the cash purse for your event and a twelve-piece throwing knife set with a golden design on the handles and a special leather carrying pouch with the same design on it as the knives, sewn together with golden thread. Denver took the cash purse and his prizes. The crowd didn't hesitate this time and began to cheer.

When the crowd was quiet, the announcer smiled from ear to ear. Announcer: Thank you very much! That is exactly what I asked of you. The third event was Staff Fighting; the winner of that event was Clay of England. Clay walked out onto the stage, silence again because the crowd was starting to become more curious what the prizes were. Announcer: Clay, I present to you, the cash purse for your event and a new staff with special carvings in it, with gold lining the inside of the carvings and a special light weight pair of gloves for better grip. Clay took the cash purse and his prizes. The crowd cheered again. The crowd again got quiet. Announcer: The forth event was Stone Throwing; the winner of that event was Louis of the Orient. Louis walked out onto the stage, the crowd snickered a little but that was all the noise they made. Announcer: Louis, I present to you, the cash purse for your event and a Clydesdale horse with a bridle and a saddle. He is a strong animal, for a strong man. Louis took the cash purse and his prizes. The crowd cheered, one even yelled that Louis needed a strong horse, but the man didn't finish his sentence. Some people laughed at this because they knew what he meant. Others gave him a dirty look for being so disrespectful.

Again, the crowd got quiet. Announcer: The fifth event was Spear Throwing; the winner of that event was Leonard of the Caribbean. Leonard walked out onto the stage, the crowd was silent. Announcer: Leonard, I present to you, the cash purse for your event and a special spear with a metal shaft instead of wood with small gems just below the spear head. This spear is perfectly balanced, so it can still be thrown with accuracy and you also get a special pair of boots made for traction. Bowen and Archer immediately recognized the spear. It was one that their mom had made a year before they left. It made them miss their mom, but they were glad to see the spear go to someone very deserving. Leonard took the cash purse and his prizes. The crowd cheered!

The crowd got quiet. Announcer: The sixth event was Bow Shooting; the winner of that event was Kenny (Kieris) of the Americas. Kieris walked out onto the stage, because Kenny was the name she had given, when she signed in for the event as a boy, the crowd again was silent. Announcer: Kenny (Kieris), I present to you, the cash purse for your event and a special bow with gold inlay down the outside edges, a leather quiver with small gems around the top and new perfectly balanced arrows. Again, Bowen and Archer recognized the bow and arrows, because they were made by their uncle Josh. Kieris took the cash purse and her prizes. The crowd cheered! Kieris joined the other winners on the opposite side of the stage from where they had started; she still had to wait until the ceremony was over before she could leave.

The crowd got quiet. Bowen and Archer had left their seats, when Kieris left the stage and were making their way toward where she was standing. Announcer: The seventh and last event was Jousting; the winner of that event was Charles of England. As Charles walked out onto the stage, Bowen and Archer had walked up to Kieris. They told Kieris that her bow and arrows were made by their uncle. Then they looked at Leonard and told him that his spear was made by their mom and as far as they knew that there were only three special spears that she had made. Then they showed him their spears. Bowen and Archer noticed that Leonard's spear wasn't made out of the same special material theirs was, but it was still special because their mom always did excellent work and she made it.

Announcer: Charles, I present to you, the cash purse for your event and a black Arabian Stallion with bridle and saddle made from the finest black leather, both trimmed in a gold design with gems. Charles took the cash purse and his prizes. The crowd stood and cheered louder than they did the whole night because the jousting event was the favorite event in these tournaments. The announcer raised his hands one last time for silence. Announcer: We want to thank all of the contestants for participating in these events and for all of you that have come out to watch these events. You have made our yearly tournament the largest we have had yet. Thank you again and good night. The tournament had taken all day and they had to light torches inside the edge of the arena for the Sumo Wrestling exhibition and the jousting event, so they could see to finish the tournament.

Bowen, Archer and Kieris said their goodbye to Charles after they let him try the special bow and arrows. They liked Charles and was hoping he was the Chosen One, but he couldn't draw it back either. They went to where James was hiding and got him. All three of them had been taking turns sneaking him food and water throughout the day, but he was glad he could now stretch his legs a little more. Because it was dark it made it easier to sneak James into the inn. While Bowen had kept an eye on James' hiding place and Kieris during the exhibition, Archer had went and rented their rooms for the night. They stayed the night in an inn with adjoining rooms. The inn keeper thought that the boys were going to share two in each room, but the boys gave Kieris one of the rooms, all to herself.

The next morning, they moved on toward the

next town called Huntington and the next tournament. They were still looking for the Chosen One, so they could give them, the bow, arrows, and help, to free this land. James: There has to be a better way and a quicker way, to find the Chosen One! Bowen: Well, if you come up with one, let us know. Archer: We should be careful, where we camp tonight. I saw those same three men pointing, at Kieris and her winnings. They were whispering, I think they may be planning, on trying to steal her money from her. When we set up camp tonight, we will have to set a little trap, for these men too. James: Maybe a little magic! Kieris: Maybe, I could do a little target practicing, with my bow and arrows? Archer: A little bit of sword play, maybe? Bowen: Anything that we do will be fun for us, but I am afraid that they will not like it. (They all laughed.) Nothing happened that night.

When they entered the town, they spotted some of the King's men, checking out everyone in the crowd, looking for the princess and the apprentice. James hid again, fearing that one of the guards would know who he was. Kieris told James, to teach her the spell, to hide who he was, so he would not have to hide anymore. James told her, that they could work on that later. It was time for the tournament to start. Archer had spotted the three men again, who had been watching Kieris at the last tournament. They had followed them here. He made sure that the others knew who they were, so they would know, what they looked like and who to watch out for. This tournament had as big a prize purse as the world one did for the noble men in the area had put up the prize money hoping that it would be big enough to make Kieris enter the contest. They hoped to catch Kieris, so they could use her against the King. Little did they know that they would not recognize who she was, even if and when they saw her?

This time the boys made sure that Kieris would be shooting last, which meant that she would win the tournament. This would make the winnings, even more tempting to the men, if they were thieves. Making them want to steal it even sooner. They did not want to have to watch over their shoulders, wondering where or when, these men would attack. Besides the large cash purse, this tournament was also different than any of the others that they had been in. It was just as large as the world, as far as merchants and bowmen that were competing, because most of the good bowmen from the world tournament had heard about this one and decided to try again. Maybe this time they would find the Chosen One. Along with that, they might also catch the thieves, if that was what they were up to. Kieris took no chances this time and shot with Bowen's bow.

Kieris pretended not to notice the three men, which were always where they could see her. Bowen, Archer and Kieris were keeping a close eye on them, without them knowing that they were. Even James decided to climb a tree with thick branches to hide in, so he could see all of them. If needed, he could always try to use some magic on the three men from there. Bowen and Archer could take care of themselves. James was not worried about himself, but he would not and could not let anything happen to Kieris. The noblemen's guards were in and around the tournament along with the King's guards. When the King's guards asked why they were there, the noblemen's guards replied that some of the noblemen wanted to supply extra security for this event because they were sponsoring it and with all of the extra people from around the world, that they thought it was necessary to protect the King's allies. They were satisfied with that answer and had no idea that this was an expensive trap to try and capture Kieris.

After they left town, they hunted for a good place to set up camp and ready their trap for the three men just in case they were thieves. They found a rock formation, that could only be climbed from the front and made Kieris a bed on the top of it, giving her a safe view point to shoot her bow and arrows from. They set up camp at the base of this rock formation, on the only side that could be climbed. They then put out all four bed rolls, using tree branches and leaves to make them look like; someone was asleep under the blankets. Since James was the weakest in fighting skills, they fixed him a place in a nearby tree, building him a platform with high edges, out of tree branches. It was the perfect place for him to watch the camp and let them know, when the thieves or anyone else arrived. Kieris and James both took their places, to wait and watch for the thieves. Bowen and Archer built a nice big fire, so it would be easier to see inside the camp and also make it easier for the thieves to find them. They found some thick brush near the camp, which they could hide in and take a nap while they waited. They were taking turns sleeping until something happened.

James spotted the men first, from his perch high in the tree. He alerted the others with his magic, making sure that they were awake and knew that the men were there. Then using his magic, he made the covers on the bed rolls move, to make them think, that they were all asleep in the beds. The men slowly moved in closer, to the three bed rolls that should have been Bowen, Archer and James, as they thought that they would be the hardest to kill and would put up a fight. They thought that Kieris, being the smallest, would also be the weakest and the easiest to kill. Just as one of the men bent over, to pull back the blanket on James bed roll, Kieris split the seat of the man's pants with an arrow that went deep into his left hip, causing him to drop his sword, bow, and arrows. He let out a loud yell in pain.

The other two plunged their swords, into
Bowen and Archer's bed rolls. Archer and
Bowen both stepped out into the light of the
campfire. Archer: Looking for us? They began
to sword fight with the other two men, while
the injured man inched his way toward his
bow and arrows, so he could help his friends.
James could not see him, to cast any spells.
Kieris had cracked her bow and could not use
it to shoot any more arrows to help them.
James could see her and the problem that she
had. The only bow and arrows that he could
see were the special ones. He cast a spell,
making them float up, onto the top of the rock,
where Kieris could reach them. Kieris saw the
thief get his bow and without looking,
accidently grabbed a special arrow, in place of
one of her own. She loaded it into the special
bow, aimed and took the shot. The arrow hit
the man, dead in his heart, killing him
instantly. By then Bowen and Archer had dealt
with the other two thieves. They would not rob
anyone else.

They heard the sound of horses coming and
were ready to fight again if they needed to.
When the horses entered the camp, the boys
could see that it was four of the King's guards.
They dismounted and looked at the three dead
men. Guard: We were afraid that these three
were going to try and rob that boy who won the
two tournaments, so we followed them. It looks
like we got here just a little too late to help
you. I am glad that none of you were hurt. We

will take these men off your hands. The guards loaded the dead men onto their horses and left. Archer as they were riding away: Thank you. I sure am glad that we didn't have to bury them. As Archer and Bowen's parents were sword and spear makers, they had also learned how to sword fight and fight with spears at a very young age too and were as good at fighting with them, as they were with the bow and arrows. They had also found other uses for them like fishing in the shallow water with the spears or using the swords to chop up meat. They just liked shooting bows better. They decided to teach James and Kieris, how to fight with these weapons too.

6: Queen Ellen

James sat in his tree perch, wondering about what he had just seen! Was she the Chosen One? He had decided that she had not come into her full power to be able to use them until the boy's lives were in danger. Kieris climbed down from the rocks and she was laughing. Bowen: What is so funny? She held up the bow and quiver of arrows.

Kieris: I guess that these belong to me now! By then, James had also joined them on the ground.

Bowen: It can't be, you could not shoot them together before. It must be a fluke! Kieris looked at him with a frown on her face. She took the bow and loaded it with one of the special arrows and pointed it at Bowen.

Kieris: Do you want to take the chance that me shooting this was only an accident? Archer stepped between her and Bowen holding up his hands to stop her from shooting.

Archer: Wait a minute! We are all friends here. You can prove that it was not a fluke or lucky shot without hurting anyone.

Kieris smiled: Sure, I just wanted to see, if he had the nerve to stand there. I would not shoot it at him anyway. James and Archer both drew a long breath of relief.

Bowen: Ok, little sister in arms. Prove that you are the Chosen One and the leader of this band. The boys set up several targets with the smallest being the size of a one-inch circle that is about the size of a hickory nut.

Archer: (He smiled at Kieris.) Ok my lady, your targets are ready for you to shoot, when you are ready!

Kieris: (She smiled.) Thank you!

Bowen: When you miss the targets, you are cooking supper this evening and cleaning up the dishes.

Kieris: No, you are cooking and cleaning, when I hit the targets! Each shot that she made was perfect, hitting the targets dead center. Archer fell down on the ground laughing.

Archer: Bowen you have to cook and do the dishes. She really got you that time. Their search was over.

Now Bowen and Archer wondered why she had not been able to shoot the bow the first time that she tried. Then they decided that it must have been because it was just not the right time for her to become the Chosen One. At least they had found the Chosen One. Now what were they going to do? Merlin had told them that they were to help the Chosen One, to free this land. None of them knew what they needed to do next. Kieris sat on a nearby stump. All the excitement of being the Chosen One was gone and had been replaced by a very sad look.

Archer: Kieris, what is wrong?

Kieris: I am the Chosen One!

Archer: I don't understand! I thought that you were happy about that?

Kieris: There is a Legend written in the scrolls, in the library in my father's castle. I have only read part of it; but if I am the Chosen One of good, truth and righteousness, then I must fight evil and correct injustices. I may have to face and destroy my father. She got up and walked off slowly, into the woods to be alone. The boys knew that this was something which she was going to have to think about, work out and get through on her own so they left her alone.

Kieris found a spot away from the boys, so they couldn't hear her cry if she needed too; but they could hear her if she yelled for help. She could not help but remember her childhood. All those memories about the King, Queen, guards, cooks, cleaning staff, the homeless and the poor: they all came flooding back to her. She remembered how Queen Ellen took care of her; how she would not let anyone else help with her care most of the time. At this time in her life, she still didn't know who her real parents were, but she was glad that she had Ellen as a mom growing up. Ellen would tell her stories about different things, some had life lessons in them, but her favorite story was when King Louie brought her home to Ellen.

Queen Ellen: Your father and I were happy for the longest time. He would go off, doing whatever he thought was best for his Kingdom. I would stay at the castle and watch over our home, the nearby villages, and entertain any guests that may come to visit, which wasn't often. He would come home and we would spend time together, but there was just something missing. Every time Ellen would tell the story, Kieris would chime in with the same questions, at the same place in the story, because she liked hearing the story as much as the Queen loved telling it.

Kieris: What was missing? Then Kieris would giggle because she already knew and loved the answer. Queen Ellen laughed: What was missing was a beautiful daughter, to love and take care of. But no matter how hard Louie and I tried we could not have a baby of our own. Then one day, your father went to check on the islands around our country, to see how they were doing. When he got to the island of Hurricane, he was very sad because everyone on the island was dead except for one little baby girl a couple months old. A plague had killed everyone else. He couldn't leave the baby there all alone, so he brought her back with him, to try to find out if she had any other family; but there was none.

Kieris giggling again: So, what did he do with the baby? Queen Ellen smiled: He brought the baby home to me, so we could be a family and wouldn't have anything missing in our lives anymore. Kieris: What did you name her? Kieris would get so excited at this point, that she couldn't sit still, so Ellen would pick her up and sit Kieris on her lap. Queen Ellen: Your father and I thought, long and hard about what to name this beautiful baby girl. She was so precious and special to us, that we thought she should have a unique name. We finally decided to name this wonderful baby girl, Kieris.

Kieris would jump off the Queen's lap, put her little hands on the sides of her face and try to act surprised. Kieris: You mean the baby girl is me? Kieris would then dance around, laughing, giggling, and clapping her hands together. It would take several minutes, for her to calm back down, so the Queen could continue, but Ellen never complained. She loved seeing Kieris so happy and even clapped along with her. Once Kieris was calmer, the Queen put her back on her lap.

At this point, Ellen would speak in a serious voice, so Kieris would know that she meant what she said, even though there was a loving smile on her face. Queen Ellen: Yes, you are the baby girl, which your father brought home to me. I have loved you, since the first time I saw you. You have filled an empty spot that was inside my heart. You have made my world, my life a brighter and warmer place. I could not love you anymore, then if I had given birth to you myself. That was Kieris's favorite part, when Ellen told her, how much she loved her.

Then Ellen would hold Kieris in her arms and rock her, while she sang first one song then another, the Queen had a voice like an angel. It wasn't long until Kieris was taking a nap or being put to bed for the night. If it was a nap, then she would wake up in Ellen's arms. They would then go for a walk, in the nearby village, the Queen loved her people. She was always doing whatever she could for them. Kieris had learned a lot from her about right and wrong, about doing unto others like you would want them to treat you. She learned that the same justice should apply to everyone rich and poor alike. She also learned that sometimes good people do bad things for a good reason and that you should never judge any one without knowing the whole story.

One day on one of their walks, a little orphan boy stole an apple from the merchant selling fruit. The boy didn't get very far and was brought back to the merchant, just as Kieris and Ellen walked by. The merchant wanted to beat the boy, for what he had done, to teach him not to steal. The Queen stopped him, she then asked the little boy why, he had stolen the apple. With tears in his eyes, he told the Queen that he took it for his little sister because she was starving and too weak to even play. The Queen turned to the merchant and told him that it wouldn't be right to beat the boy for trying to save his sister. Instead the boy would come and work for him; he would clean the merchant's store and make deliveries that way the merchant could stay open and sell more goods and the boy could earn food for him and his sister. Everyone working together and no one suffering for it, in fact they all would gain.

The merchant had dropped his head in shame that he hadn't taken the time to find out why. Then he thanked the Queen for her thoughtful and wise words. He turned to the boy, gave him two apples, one for his sister and one for himself and then told the boy to be there first thing in the morning to work. As the boy was leaving and told him to bring his sister with him, that she could rest in the back room while he worked until she felt better and so she would be safe. Several weeks later, the merchant ended up adopting both the boy and girl.

Even though Queen Ellen had come from a wealthy family, her father had taught her that a happy person is a more loyal and productive person. That other people have feelings too and you must show everyone respect if you want them to show you respect, no matter their social standing. He also told Ellen that there were some, who no matter how good you were to them, would always act badly but that was no excuse to ever treat them badly. He also believed that everyone should be able to hunt and take care of themselves if they needed to, so he also taught Ellen how to shoot a bow.

Ellen had been teaching these same lessons, through stories and by being an example, like she did with the merchant and the boy. At this time, Kieris had gotten big enough to pull back a child size bow, so the Queen began to teach Kieris how to shoot. Kieris picked up the basics quickly always trying to learn more, so she could do better. She loved the Queen and wanted Ellen to be proud of her. It wasn't too long until she could shoot almost as well as the Queen. Instead of taking a nap after lunch, she would practice shooting her bow. Life was so wonderful back then.

7: Secrets

One day, right after Kieris turned twelve, the Queen died. Kieris mourned the loss of the only mother she had ever known. The King didn't spend a lot of time with her and the Queen as she was growing up. Now that the Queen was gone, the King demanded that she stay inside the castle for her own safety. He would also expect her to have all her meals with him, except when he had a meeting or was away. Kieris now was practicing shooting the Queen's bow, which she had left her, almost all day. It was the only thing that she was allowed to do that brought her any joy.

On days she could not go outside to practice because of the weather. She wondered through the castle looking for anything to do. Sometimes she would help the maids clean, other times she would go into the kitchen and help the cooks. In return the cooks taught her how to prepare some of her favorite foods and the maids showed her a secret tunnel. Now when the King was home, and the weather was bad, she would sneak around and follow him to see if he would lead her to any more secret tunnels. There were several tunnels, some were connected and led to different places, such as the kitchen, library and the throne room. There was one in the throne room that connected to the King's chambers; it also went outside of the castle walls, as an escape tunnel.

One day while she was following him, she saw him open a new secret place in the throne room. She had to wait for him to go on one of his trips to check this one out. In the meantime, the King was becoming more controlling. Saying that she should be taking riding lessons and learn more lady like things, such as entertaining guests. He would tell her; someday she would be the Queen and would be expected to do the Queen's duties. He told her how beautiful she was becoming and as soon as she was old enough that she would be married. She would ask him to whom, but he would always say that they would talk about it when the time came.

When he was home, she would take riding lessons. She didn't mind riding because she did like horses and they seemed to like her, but there was not much room inside the castle grounds to really ride like she wanted to. No matter how much she asked, the King always said no to her riding outside the castle grounds. She was feeling more and more like a caged bird, a prisoner in her own home. The only time she got to practice with her bow now, was when he was away.

Once while he was away, she sneaked out of the castle through the tunnels, to visit one of the guards, who had been kind to her. He had a broken leg and was not able to do any work. She was shocked to find him half starved. He had gotten the broken leg protecting the King, but since he could not work, the King had refused to pay him. She went back in the castle and discreetly took some food from the kitchen back to the guard. She even cleaned his house and helped him as much as she could until he was well enough to take care of himself.

When the guard was well enough to return to work, he told a few of the other nice guards what she had done. They decided to repay her kindness by teaching her to fight with a staff and a sword. They also included her in their bow practices. She had gotten so much better at shooting that the King's best bowman could not beat her in a match. Of course, they could only do these things when the King was away with his meaner guards. For the most part, the guards were kind gentle souls, which would only fight if they had to. The King's special guards that he would always take with him, were cruel and mean to everyone, except Kieris. They weren't nice or kind to her, but they were not cruel either because they didn't want the King mad at them.

She finally had a chance to check out the secret place that she saw the King open in the throne room. When she opened it, the thrown itself moved to one side and revealed a door. She went inside and found out that it was a secret room, to hide and listen to others talking in the throne room. One day while she was in the secret room, some of the mean guards came in the throne room and were talking about her. They were saying how beautiful she was becoming, that if it wasn't for the King, there were some vile things that they would like to do to her.

Kieris was disgusted with what she was hearing and was about to cover her ears, when one of the guards said something about her parents. She listened closer as they were talking about how they and the King had killed everyone on Hurricane Island except her. How the King covered it up saying the plague killed everyone. The King was evil but smart; he even had the beautiful Kieris fooled. Kieris was glad when they left the room, she could not stand any more of their talk. It was evil, cruel, and vulgar, it made her scared and mad about all these things. What else did she not know about this man, that she had been calling father. From that point on she was extra careful around the King and his evil guards, but she could not let on that she knew anything because that would put her in more danger.

She had become good friends with the nice guards. One time while the King and his special guards were away, on one of their raiding trips, she talked the nice guards into letting her ride outside the castle. They agreed but only if she wore a hooded cloak, so no one would recognize her, because they were afraid, not only what he would do to them but to her, if he ever found out. She told them that she understood, put on a cloak, and promised to be careful. So, she rode to the nearby village she had visited as a child, with the Queen.

She could not believe her own eyes. The village was run down and falling apart. The people looked half-starved and sickly. This was the real reason the King didn't want her to come out of the castle. He had not harmed the villages next to the castle before, so the Queen wouldn't find out. Now he was trying to keep her a prisoner, so she would not find out how evil he was. She passed an apple orchard on her way back to the castle that was for the King only. She picked as many apples as she could carry and took them back to the village. The boy that the Queen saved remembered her. She told the villagers that they must never let the King, or his guards know what she has done to help them, or the King might lock her away so she couldn't help them again.

When she got back to the castle, she sneaked into the storage rooms and could not believe how much food was there; some had been there so long that it was beginning to rot. Over time, she snuck part of the villager's food back to them. The cooks, maids and nice guards caught on to what she was doing and decided to help. Whenever they saw or heard of someone in need, they would come to her and ask what she wanted to do to help. Most of the time, she would take care of it herself, but if the King was home, they would sneak things out for her to the people.

One of the guards told her about a little girl from the orphanage that he saw shivering in the street. He had gotten her a warm cup of cocoa from one of the merchants and took her back to the orphanage. Kieris had asked how big the girl was and which village that he had been in. He told her, then she went to her closet and pulled out one of her old coats that she had outgrown and gave it to the guard, to take to the little girl because she had received word that the King would be back that day. The guard said he would, thanked Kieris for her kindness and left.

That evening after the King came home, one of the cooks told Kieris all about this young boy who had wondered into her village, his family had been killed by the evil guards, the only reason he survived was his father told him to hide. He loved animals and would rather stay outside with them, than go to the orphanage. Kieris told the cook to get one of the nice guards, to help her sneak the boy into the castle and take him to the stables, when she thought it was safe, then she would go talk to the boy. The cook nodded her head yes and left, as the King walked into the room.

King: What was that about? Kieris: She just wanted to know what we wanted her to fix for our guests when they arrived. I had received word while you were gone, that there were a few young men that wanted to come speak with us both. There is a Duke, a Prince and a Lord coming. They will each arrive a week apart from each other. The King laughed, for he had no intentions of anyone having her except him. Kieris looked at him funny, so he covered his tracks. King: I told you, my beautiful Kieris, that you would be a Queen and come your next birthday, you will be old enough to marry and you will be Queen.

Kieris: Is that why you think they are coming? They don't know me or have never met me. Why would they want to marry me, unless it's just for the crown? The King laughed again: No, that is why I am back early. Even though I have kept you inside the castle to protect you, stories of your beauty have spread to other countries. They are coming to see if the stories are true and possibly ask my permission to marry you, if they like you. Kieris: What if I don't like them and don't want to marry them? King: Oh, my sweet princess, I wish you could choose your husband, but you are obligated to do what is best for this country, so you will marry who I say is worthy and no one else. Do you understand? Kieris thought she did and nodded her head yes.

Kieris made up an excuse and left the room. She still had to talk to the boy and decide how to help him before supper. Then she would worry about the young men that were coming.

She was careful not to be seen by the King or the evil guards, as she went to the stable. When she walked in, the boy was curled up in the stall with her favorite horse, taking a nap. Kieris did not have the heart to wake him up. She told Fred, the man in charge of the stables, to keep the boy out of sight, let him help with the horses, and to teach him which of the guards he could trust and the ones he couldn't. Kieris told Fred that she would return to check on the boy, when it was safe for her to do so; and then decide what to do about him. The man agreed; he always needed and could always use more help.

With the King watching her more than normal and the preparations for their visitors, she wasn't able to go back to the stables for three days. She was very pleased that the boy was looking much healthier. Kieris watched for a minute, as the boy worked with one of the horses. He was teaching it to bow. Fred spotted her and walked over. Fred: Princess Kieris, the boy has been a great help to me, both here and at my home, no troubles with him at all, he is wonderful with the horses and we have hit it off very well. I haven't said anything to the boy, but if it pleases you and if the boy agrees, I would like to adopt him. Kieris smiled at him. She had already thought; if there were no problems, that the boy would stay here, but he was too young still to go without supervision. Kieris was glad that Fred wanted to adopt him and watch out for him. She giggled a moment, because the thought crossed her mind, that the boy could even teach Fred a few things that he didn't already know about the horses.

Fred and Kieris, walked over to the boy, when he saw her, he bowed. Kieris laughed: There is no need to bow to me in the stables. Save it for when there are others around. I see you have a way with horses.

Boy: I have a way with all animals, but I love horses the most. Thank you for having them and bringing me here. I was so sad and lost when my family was murdered, I was helpless and couldn't do anything. Fred helped me see that it wasn't my fault. I would like to stay with the horses here in the stable, if it is ok. Kieris smiled at the boy, maybe this would not be difficult at all.

Kieris: Fred and I have been talking. He says you are a great help. I think you could teach Fred a few things about horses. (She giggles again.) But a stable is a place for horses to live, not people. The boy went to interrupt her when she put up a hand to silence him. Kieris: Hear me out before you say anything, because when I am done, you will have a choice to make. I understand you have been staying with Fred, that you two have been getting along very well. Fred has also told me, that he would be proud and honored, if you would allow him to adopt you, he doesn't want to take your father's place, but to be there to guide you, if you need it. You are still a little too young to be on your own, so your choices are; go to the orphanage and possibly get a job in the village taking care of the animals there, or allow Fred to adopt you, listen to his guidance, and work here in the stables with him.

The boy was speechless; it was a lot to take in at once, to be adopted and to be given a choice. Kieris: I will be back as soon as I can safely do so. You and Fred can talk it over and you can give me your answer then. Fred, I want you to tell him what would be expected of him and explain to him what you are offering in the way of guidance. If he is to make this decision, he needs to know all the facts and consequences of his decision, regardless what he chooses. Fred and the boy both agreed. She left and went to her room to get ready for supper with the King.

As she was getting ready, she was thinking about decisions she would have to make soon. There were only two reasons she had not run away already; one, she wasn't sure where she could go and be safe; and two, she wouldn't be here to help the people. She thought she knew what he meant by best for the country; he meant the best for himself. If he thought that she would stand by and allow him to marry her off to someone like him, he has seriously wrong. Then she had thought about possibly making allies with her visitors if they weren't like the King.

That is part of the reason when the King would have his tournaments, she would sneak out and shoot in the bow portion of it. To meet new people and hopefully make some allies, and of course to see if she could find some competition, the guards had become way too easy to beat. She knew that she could never finish a tournament because then the King would find out what she was doing. So, she would have one of the nice guards to pull her out, if she was in danger of being caught or if the tournament was near the end.

Over the next several weeks, suitors came and went, at least as far as she knew. If one of them showed any interest in her or asked for her hand, the King would have them killed somewhere just outside his Kingdom after they left. The others he would just let them leave with no harm to them, so it would throw people off that he had anything to do with them dying. She had also talked to Fred and the boy during those weeks and the boy agreed to Fred adopting him. They were doing great and were planning on doing a little show with the horses at the next tournament.

8: Family

Now she would not get to see the show, because she was on another adventure. After shooting against Bowen and Archer, she thought they would make great allies, so she had followed them to the next town. So much had happened since then, she knew the right thing to do was go against the King, she wasn't sure exactly yet how she would do this, but this time she had some real allies. When she finally returned, it was daylight and the boys had already packed up the camp. They moved on toward the next town.

There, they ran into the King's guards again. When they entered the town, they saw that the King's guards were still looking for the wizard's apprentice and the princess but this time, they were also collecting taxes. The boys had never been in town and seen them do this before. They were cruel, beating people and throwing families out into the street, with no place to go. It did not make any difference, if there were children or old people, if they could not pay the King's high taxes; they were cast out to die of hunger and the lack of shelter.

Kieris watched the guards with tears in her eyes. She had given all her prize money, to families to save their homes, but did not have enough money to help them all. Kieris: I don't know how my father could be so cruel and heartless toward little children, after all he adopted me. He was not at all like that when the Queen was alive.

James: I am sorry you had to see that. Don't cry, we will help you make things right. The guards left and soon it was time for the tournament to start. While Kieris, Bowen and Archer competed in the bow shooting contest, James talked to some of the townspeople, about what they had seen. The taxes were only collected once a year and based on how many people lived in the house. The townspeople had taken in families, who had lost their homes, but hid the fact of how many were actually living, in each house from the guards. They feared that the King would have the whole town burned to the ground if he found out. He also found out that Merlin had been arrested and put in prison.

That made him wonder, why they were still looking for him. One of the older women in the town had told him that the King had gone mad. The rumor was that after the Queen had died that he had fallen in love with the princess, his adopted daughter. The King had watched her grow up; she had gotten more beautiful with every year that passed. He had tried to keep her locked up and away from other men until she had gotten old enough to marry. She had been visited by a prince or two this past year who had asked the King for her hand in marriage. She did not love any of them, but the King feared that she would run away with one of them, so he ordered his guards to kill all of them. With her missing, his reign of terror had grown worse. After the tournament, they left the town and moved on toward the next town; along the way they met an old man.

The old man: Don't go into town! Don't let anyone see you, the guards are killing men, hide! Hide! I have to hide! Mark my words, if you go into town, they will kill you! He ran off into the woods.

Bowen: That man has gone mad. What he was saying doesn't make any since. Why would the guards be killing all the men that they see? The guards are men themselves!

Archer: Crazy or not, there has been too many strange things going on here lately not to check it out. We don't want to take any chances with Kieris.

They made camp for the night, in a well-hidden spot. Bowen started teaching Kieris, how to fight with a sword and Archer started teaching James, how to fight with a staff. After an hour of practice, they switched and Bowen was teaching James, to fight with a sword. Archer was teaching Kieris, how to fight with a staff. Bowen and Archer both were surprised that Kieris already knew the basics and was picking up the advanced lessons quickly. James, of course, was having trouble with getting his stance down right, much less holding the weapon correctly. They would sleep in shifts again tonight, until they found out what was going on. The old man may have been crazy, or the King could have gone completely mad; either way they could not take any chances.

James would sneak into the town after dark that night and see what he could find out. The first thing that he noticed was; there were no men in town and no boys, over the age of five or six years. He found a poster on the side of one of the buildings; he took it down and put it into his pocket, so he could show it to the others. He talked to an old lady who hid him for a while; because the guards were searching the house beside her, for men. They had already searched hers and didn't find any. She told him how part of the guards had deserted, hiding in the woods with their sons, to protect them. No male was safe from the King's madness. He was going to keep all men away from Kieris, even if he had to kill them to do it.

As soon as James could safely leave town, he went back to their hidden camp. Bowen: Well, what did you find out?

James: That old man was not crazy. The King ordered that all the guards be turned into eunuchs.

Archer: What is a eunuch?

James: They are men, who have had their manly parts removed, so they cannot make love to a woman. The ones who have refused are either counted as traitors to their country and are hiding out with their sons to save them or have been killed. A lot of the soldiers have left the King's guard to save themselves and their sons. The problem with that is; it leaves their wives and daughters at the mercy of the guards who still work for the King.

This new law that the King passed, states that all males in the country have to become a eunuch or be killed. This law affects every male over the age of ten years. He wants Kieris returned to him and this done to all men, so they can never be with her. The order is plain, be changed or die!

Kieris: He has gone completely mad! Archer had just finished reading the poster that James had handed him.

Archer: Yes! He is mad. No, he is not mad, he is crazy! He wants to marry his own daughter! Kieris, he wants to marry you! That is just sick!

Kieris dropped her head: He is not my father! I am adopted! He lied to me and told me that my parents were killed by a plague, shortly after I was born. He told the Queen the same lie, that he had found me and that my parents died in a plague, on the island of Hurricane.

As I grew older, I overheard the guards talking about the raids that they had made on the island of Hurricane and the people that they had killed there. I heard them talking about my real parents. I was spared, only because the Queen wanted children and could not have any of her own. They stole everything from the island of Hurricane; food, weapons, and anything else that they could find to use or to sell. After the Queen died, he did not want me out of his sight. The older I got, the more he tried to keep me like a prisoner. He kept telling me that someday I would be a Queen. He just did not tell me that he was planning on making me his queen. Kieris looked like she was going to be sick.

Bowen: There was no plague, on the island of Hurricane?

Kieris: The only plague there was the King and his guards murdering everyone; and stealing from those they murdered.
Archer: Do you know what your real parents' names were?

Kieris: Yes! My real parents' names were Joshua and Chasity Carnes.

Bowen: Why did we not see it before? She has mom's blond hair.

Archer: She has dad's blue eyes.

Kieris: What? What are you two talking about?

Bowen looked at her: Hi little sister! My name is Bowen Carnes and I am your brother. He is Archer Carnes and he is your brother too.

Archer: When we left home, you had not been born yet, but you were due any day. We did not know if we had a brother or a sister. Then when we heard that our parents died in the plague, we thought that you did too.

Bowen: We are so glad that you are alive, and we are all together. They all hugged. Even James got in on the hugging.

Kieris was crying. Kieris: I am so happy that I have a real family.

Archer: Yes, and a family; protects each other.

Bowen: We will avenge our parents' murders too.

James: Let us decide what to do now. They are killing men and boys; so, unless you want to become a eunuch, we can't even get close to the King.

James: To safeguard us, we need to change what people see, when they look at us. Kieris you are first! In truth and light let Bowen, Archer and I see you as you are; but to others when they look at you, let them see a homely woman, beyond your years with sad brown eyes and auburn hair.

Kieris: Now you James! To Bowen, Archer and I let us see you in truth and light, but to others who look at you, only let them see an old gray headed woman, feeble and slow. James smiled at her.

Bowen: How do we know, if it worked or not. James walked over and looked at his reflection, in the still clear water of the spring, near where they were camped. It showed him as an old gray headed woman.

James: Ok ladies, what would you like for others to think that you look like? (James and Kieris laughed.) Bowen and Archer did not think that it was funny.

Archer: What do you mean ladies? He pointed his sword at James and Kieris, with Bowen stepping in between Archer and them.

Kieris: You said you would keep me safe and avenge our parents' deaths. Your only choices are to become a eunuch, be killed, or just let others think that you are something that you are not when they look at you. If they see a weak but beautiful woman, she might be able to get next to the King. A pretty woman could even get close to the King; maybe even close enough to kill him.

Bowen: She is right, but we need help. The King is still a very powerful man, even if he is crazy.

Archer: He is crazy, so why not drive him even crazier? James, I want to be seen in others eyes; the same as Kieris looks in real life.

Bowen smiled: That is a great idea! James, would you make me look like Kieris, too?

James: Two women who look as beautiful as Kieris is, if that don't confuse him then nothing will. Kieris was flattered by the description that James had used to describe her.

Kieris: Thanks James!

James: I don't think you want me to make you look like Kieris yet because all the guards would be trying to take you back to the King. If you avoided them, then there would still be the men who are out for the reward money that the King has offered. I think we better wait until we are inside the castle to do that. Bowen and Archer agreed to wait.

Bowen: Make us both just plain women. I would hate to have to punch any man who tried to get fresh with me. They all laughed.

9: Army

Archer: I think I know where and how we can get some help.

James: Where and how? Kieris smiled: The enemy of my enemy is my friend. Archer: Right! The guards that deserted the King's army and their sons!

Bowen: You are right, the guards that deserted and their sons may be willing to fight. They would be fighting for their own freedom, their families, and their own lives. They would be fighting, to free this land from a crazy King.

Kieris: That is a great idea!

James: Now all we have to do is find them and get them to agree to fight.
Kieris: I think I know how to get them to help, but we must all look like our real selves.
James: Guys, I guess you get to look like yourselves, for a while longer.

Bowen: Let's move to higher ground, I have an idea about how we can find them. Look for smoke, just as it is getting day light. They will have to build fires at night to keep warm and cook for the next day since smoke from a fire during the day would let the other guards, who are still with and loyal to the King, know where they are located. That is how we will find out where their camp is.

Archer: Kieris, now we know who, but how are you going to get them to help us?

Kieris: I am going to offer them a ruler, who will be kind, fair, and show justice to all the people, not just a few. I will offer pardons, for their crimes against the people and a better way of life. I will give them a Queen to rule them, in place of the cruel crazy King which they have now.

James: It is worth a try; and if it doesn't work, then the two Carnes brothers, can always take their shot at taking away the Kings throne.

Kieris: It will work; most of the guards know and like me. I have helped some of them in the past. They will know that I am telling them the truth.

Archer: What if, when they see you, all they see is a way to turn you in? To give you to the King, hoping that would put an end to all of this madness?

Kieris: I will remind them that the King will always fear that I will be with some other man; so, turning me in will not stop just how crazy the King has become!

Bowen: First things first! We have to find the guards and their sons; then we'll worry about getting them to help us.

James: When we do find them and before we enter the camp, I will turn you all back, so they can see who you really are.

Kieris: Thank you! It is time for me to grow up and do whatever I can to help these people.

Bowen: Kieris, our parents would be very proud of you and what you are trying to do.

Archer: Little sister, we are both proud of you too. The four of them climbed to the top, of a nearby hill. They all watched in different direction, as dawn broke for signs of smoke.

James: There it is! There is the smoke and that will be where the camp is located.
Archer: It looks to be about five miles to the east and a lot deeper into the woods.

Bowen: Ok! Let us go find some help! They started walking in the direction that they had seen the smoke before the guards had put it out to hide their location from the other guards and others who might be hunting for them.

The farther they walked, the thicker the trees and brush got. They didn't want to leave an easy trail for the King's guards to follow, when it finally crossed their minds to look for the runaway guards like they had; so, they had to change directions a few times to get through the brush. That evening they found a place to camp and would look for signs of smoke again in the morning, just to make sure that they were still going in the right direction. They would have to make sure their fire was out early too. While James and Archer set up camp, Bowen and Kieris went hunting for food.

Bowen had seen her skills with a bow in the tournament, but hunting was different. Besides he wanted to know if she was okay, because he didn't think she had ever killed anyone before the thieves had attacked. After they were out of hearing distance from the camp, Kieris stopped Bowen and motioned toward a fallen log for them to sit on. After they sat down, Bowen began to laugh.

Kieris: What is so funny?

Bowen: Here we haven't gone very far, and you already need a rest. Kieris hit him on the arm: No, I wanted to talk to you in private. Why did you ask me to hunt with you instead of Archer?

Bowen: Because shooting targets and hunting are different. Kieris smiled: Yes, they are. I have gone on two hunts before with the nice guards from the King's castle, when they were trying to help me get more food for the villagers. I hesitated the first time I shot at an animal. It was a deer, I didn't make a kill shot because I hesitated, and the animal suffered more because of it. It bothered me to kill the animal, but it bothered me more that it suffered like that. But the guards helped me through that and now I only shoot animals if I am sure I have a kill shot. But that can't be the only reason that you asked me to go hunting. You have been watching me with this worried look on your face for the past day or so.

Bowen: There is another reason I asked you to go hunting. I wanted to talk to you in private too. I knew that it bothered me and Archer the first time we had to kill someone, but we got through it together. I know you are a tough young lady, sis, and you are used to doing and dealing with things by yourself; but Archer and I are your brothers and we are here for you. We both want you to know that you can come to us with anything; that you can depend on us. Kieris: I know this in my heart, but you're right it is hard for me to confide or depend on anyone. Just have patience with me on that.

Bowen: We will but I need to ask. Was that the first time you had to kill someone, you know when you shot the thief? Kieris dropped her head and spoke so softly that Bowen could barely hear her say yes. Bowen put his arm around her and then she lifted her head and had tears in her eyes.

Kieris: I have tried to put it out of my mind, but every time it keeps coming back and gnawing at me. It didn't bother me to shoot him in the butt. I know I did what I had to, to protect you and Archer but it still makes me feel like I did something wrong. Will I ever feel better or will this gnaw at me the rest of my life?

Bowen: You know how you didn't want the animal you hunted to suffer but needed to kill it for food. You got through that because you knew it was the right thing to do even though you really didn't want to harm the animals. It is the same thing; you wounded him by shooting him in the butt, but that didn't stop him. He didn't give you much of a choice, either you kill him or let him kill Archer or me, if not both of us. Then he still could have hurt you and James after that. Sometimes good people have to do bad things for good reasons. It will always bother you to have to kill someone, but if it is for the right reason and there is no way to avoid it, you will learn to live with your decisions. It hurts because you have a good heart, sis. If it didn't hurt, then I would be more worried about you.

She nodded that she understood, then cried on his shoulder for a little while. When she was done, she wiped the tears away.

Kieris: Thank you, Bowen. I am glad you and Archer are here for me. If either of you ever need to talk; I will be here for you also. Archer and James are going to start worrying about us. We need to find some food and get back soon. Bowen was glad that his sister had opened up to him. He didn't want her to suffer over saving all of their lives. They each got two rabbits and found some berries and wild onions and then went back to camp.

When Archer saw them coming, he began to laugh.

James: What is so funny?

Archer: Just watch. Kieris and Bowen came into camp, laid down the food and sat down.

Kieris: We got the food now you two can cook it. Bowen and Kieris laughed.

Archer: You were gone so long I thought you would be dragging a big deer behind you. So little sis had to teach you how to hunt for rabbits? Archer and James both laughed.

Bowen sounded serious: Next time, you get to go hunting in these woods and tell me how easy it is to shoot anything in this thick brush. Besides she got two rabbits and I got two, we are both good hunters. Bowen looked at Kieris and they both started laughing.

Kieris: I see, my two brothers like to pick and joke with each other. Just remember if you pick on me, I do know how to pick back; so be warned. They all laughed.

Archer cleaned the rabbits and James cooked them with the onions. They all ate and went to bed early. They would have to get up real early to check for smoke. Kieris slept a little better that night. It had helped talking to Bowen and knowing she could count on her brothers. Having brothers was going to be great, except when they get around to picking on her, but she would be prepared for that. James had also noticed that something was bothering her right after she shot the thief and had been worried about her too, but she seemed to be doing better now. So, they all had a good reason to rest a little easier tonight. All except Archer, who was sleeping lightly, Bowen hadn't had a chance to tell him about his and Kieris's talk. Even though they were farther away from human danger, there was still danger here, from big cats, bears and they didn't know exactly how close they were or weren't from the runaway guard's camp.

They got up early the next morning and checked for smoke. They were a little bit off course but were still basically going in the right direction. They ate, broke camp, and started their journey again. Archer figured that it should only take about half a day to get to the guard's camp; as long as they didn't run into any more thick brush. After a long walk, they ran into one of the guard's sons. He was about twelve years old and was in the woods setting rabbit traps, to help with their need for food. Kieris had hidden her face, because she was not ready to let anyone see her. The boy ran for help. James had already turned them all back, so they would be seen as themselves. They kept walking in the direction, that they had seen the boy run. Soon they were met by six big men. James: Hi! We came to join your fight! They were all taken into the camp, in front of all the other guards and their sons.

The leader of the camp was named Robert. Robert: What fight? We are just trying to protect our sons.

Archer: Hi! My name is Archer. I know that some of you will remember me from the tournaments and you have also seen my brother Bowen there.
Bowen: Your children are not safe! I know that you are just trying to protect your sons, but what about your wives and daughters. A lot of them have been cast out into the streets to starve; some of them beaten and some of them have even been killed.

Archer: This is all happening, because you are not there to protect them. Even your sons, who are here with you, they are still not safe either. We found you and the men who still work for the King will too. We come to offer you a way out, which will ensure the safety of your whole families.

Bowen: This way out is not free. You will have to fight for it! You will have to fight for your freedom, your lives, and the lives of your families. You would have to fight to end the rule of a King who has gone crazy and replace him with a ruler who will bring peace to this land.

Robert: I guess you want us to help kill the King and now you want to be our King, a stranger from another land.

Bowen: No! My brother and I don't want to be your King. We are here to fight for a ruler to replace that crazy King. Replace him with a ruler who can bring peace to this land. Someone, who will help the people and protect them, not try to hurt them. Another guard speaks up!
Shawn: Who? Make one of you as our leader? You a stranger from another land or maybe you are talking about the wizard's apprentice?

James: NO! Not me! What about a leader who is one of your own? Someone you all know and love. Someone who has always shown kindness, to everyone and who has even helped some of you in the past!

Robert: The only one I know like that was the Princess Kieris and she left us to save herself. We can't blame her for that. We all wish that we all could escape.

James: Would you fight for her? Would you fight to make her your ruler? Would you serve her, if she was your Queen?

Archer: Kieris is everything that you said this country needs. Kind to everyone and would give justice to everyone. She would risk her own life to save others and she is truthful in everything that she says and does.

Shawn: She would make a good ruler, but she is not here, and we will not take a chance on losing our sons. Kieris had cleaned up, changed clothes, and now looked like a princess. She was still keeping herself covered, so they could not tell who she was.

Kieris: What about losing your wives, daughters and still remaining traitors? You could still lose your sons and your own lives. I am here and if you will fight to save this country to make a better way of life for everyone; I will stand and fight with you. I offer you peace in this land, pardons, living with your whole families, lower taxes, truth, and fair justice for everyone.

First man, Thomas: Who are you, to offer these things to us? Kieris steps forward and uncovers her head to let the people know who she is and that she was there.

Kieris: I am Kieris, your princess, and what I want to know is will you fight for a Queen who will give you all these things? Thomas knelt down on one knee and lowered his head looking at the ground: You're Highness! You will go against your father?

Kieris: I will go against any man, royal or common, that would starve children, break up homes and kill innocent people. Anyone who would make children homeless or orphans! I ask you again, will you fight for your freedom, your children, your own families, and for a better way of life. Will you fight to make me your Queen?

All the men and boys in the camp; went down on one knee and in one voice cried out: Death to the King! Long live Queen Kieris! We pledge our alliance and lives to the service of our Queen. Long live our Queen!

Kieris: We have our army! Now we need a plan of attack. Arise everyone; we must work together to save our land. James: I have an idea! I can't change, what all of them look like to others at one time, but I can a few at a time.

10: The Plan

Archer: Yes, all the ladies of the village can prepare a great feast to honor the King. The men all looked at Archer as if he had lost his mind.

Kieris laughed: Gather around and I will explain what they are talking about. James, I am going to need your help to show them what we mean by changing them. First change me so they will know that the spell does not hurt or really change you.

James: Watch Kieris! In truth and light hide Kieris' identity from their sight; make her a boy but only for a minute in their sight, then return her so they can see her as herself. She changed what she looked like in their sight. She now looked like a boy, but her voice remained the same.

Thomas: Do you mean that you can cast a spell on me, that no matter who looked at me, they would see the King?

Archer: Yes! But since so many people hate the King and want to kill him, I don't think I would want them to see the King when they looked at me!

Bowen: Me either! They all laughed.

Thomas: I see your point.

Kieris: Ok, here is the plan. James will change you, a few at a time. You will look the same to everyone here in the camp. To other people, other guards, and even to your wives and daughters, you will look like other girls and women. You will have to work on making yourselves, sound like girls and women, since the spell will not change your voices. Remember, they are not hunting girls or women to kill them. The plan is to make the King think that all of us women are having him a party to celebrate his marriage to Kieris and that we are bringing his bride back home to him or should I say brides back to him. James will you please!

James: Show this group what the King will see when he looks at Bowen and Archer, but only for a minute! Watch Bowen and Archer! James began to chant, as they watched Bowen and Archer. What the group then saw were two girls who looked exactly like Kieris.

Bowen started acting like a fool: Oh King, I am Kieris, marry me! Archer chimed in on the fun: No King, I am Kieris, marry me! The camp laughed as the boys changed back into their true selves.

Thomas: Homely brides! They all laughed again.

Kieris: Well, do you think that the boys could

get close enough to the King to capture him?

David, the second man: Capture him! Why not kill him? He would kill us, if he had the chance.

Kieris: Because we are not the King! We will give him what he has denied all of us; a fair trial. You want a leader who is fair and just. That must apply to everyone. The guilty and the innocent a like! The people will judge him, all the people. He will be sentenced, according to the verdict, of the people or do you want a ruler who plays favorites, who is cruel and unjust, like the King that you already have? He has done a lot of bad things and he must answer for these crimes, in a fair and just manner.

Archer: You are all afraid, for the lives of your children and your parents. The King killed my parents and I want to see him dead, but vengeance is not the answer. He must die by the will of all the people, for his crimes. His punishment must be by the law. If we do not go by the law, then the innocent people like all of you, who betrayed the King to protect your families would be found guilty and killed. Why something happened is just as important, as who did it!

Bowen: We can fight and win this battle, but we can't have a better country, if we do this out of hate and vengeance. We must fight this battle, out of love for our families, for this country, for a new ruler and a better way of life. Fight for a new ruler, who will be fair and just, to all the people. (He knelt down on one knee.) We must fight for our new Queen Kieris. Kieris as my Queen, I pledge to you my sword, my loyalty, and my life, to serve you and this country.

Archer: (He too knelt down on one knee.) Kieris as my Queen, I pledge to you my sword, my loyalty, and my life, to serve you and this country. All the men and their sons in the camp, knelt down on one knee and pledged their swords, loyalty, and lives, to serve their new Queen Kieris and this new country. That is all, except James. No one noticed, that he did not accept Kieris as his Queen and pledge his life and loyalty to her as such. They all got back to their feet and yelled, long live the Queen. Long live Kieris our Queen. Kieris moved off to herself, while the men built a fire, cooked supper, and ate. She had a lot on her mind.

She had lost her real parents, but then she had never really known them, because she was only days old when the King had killed them. She was about to lose the only father, that she had ever known. She had found two brothers, who would give their lives to protect her. Then there was James? He was a good friend, but she had noticed that he did not pledge loyalty to her or the country, this troubled her.

Archer brought her a plate of food: You are my Queen now, but first you are my sister. What is wrong?

Kieris: As your Queen right now, I have a lot on my mind, to worry and think about. As your sister, I am worried about James. He did not pledge his loyalty to me or to this country.

Archer: What would you like for me to do about it, as your brother?

Kieris smiled at him: Just see if you can find out why and let me know. He smiled at her.

Archer: Ok! Now eat, you will need all your strength for what lies ahead. Kieris ate and lay down to rest but found it hard to sleep. When she finally went to sleep, Archer got Bowen alone and told him about James. They both went hunting for James and found him on the river bank alone, just sitting there watching the clear water as it hit the larger stones in the river and made waves as it passed just below where he was sitting.

The boys wanted to talk to him alone, so the others would not know, what was going on or hear what they were saying. This was the perfect spot for that. Archer: Hi, do you mind if we join you?

James: No! It is so peaceful here, a place to sit and think.

Bowen: We wanted to talk to you alone. James: Ok!

Archer: James do you think that Kieris will make a good Queen?

James: I think that she will make a great Queen!

Bowen: Do you think that everyone who pledged their lives and loyalty to her and this country will keep their pledges?

James: Yes! They would be fools if they didn't.

Archer: That is enough. What I want to know is why you didn't pledge your life and loyalty to the new Queen?

James: I was hoping that no one had noticed.

Bowen: No one did notice except Kieris and it worried her. She thinks a lot of you.

James: That is the problem. I love Kieris! If I pledge my service, my life and loyalty to her as my Queen, then there can never be anything more between us. I will only be her wizard; bound to her, the way Merlin was bound to the King. I don't think my heart could stand never being anything more than a wizard to her.

Archer smiled: I thought so, but I had to make sure that was the reason.

Bowen: What if you pledge to Kieris not as the Queen. What if you pledge to her, your love and protection? Pledge as a man to the woman that he loves, not as a wizard.

James: I need to talk to her alone, but I am afraid to. If she doesn't love me and accept my pledging as a boyfriend, then there is no chance for us to ever be anything else! He paused.

Archer: Don't worry. I know she has feelings for you. Don't give up so easily. He smiled at James and patted him on the back. Archer and Bowen left James alone, to think about what he was going to say to Kieris.

Archer returned to Kieris to report to her, as her brother, what he had found out about James. Archer: Kieris, are you awake?

Kieris: Yes. I have too much on my mind to sleep. Come in. Archer entered the tent where Kieris was and sat down beside her on the bed. Kieris: Well, what did you find out?
Archer: I found out that he would die, to keep you from being hurt. Kieris looked like she was really puzzled!

Kieris: Then why would he not pledge his allegiance to me as his Queen?
Archer: Did you know that if he pledges his allegiance to you as his Queen, then he can

only serve you as your wizard? Just like Merlin served the King! He does not see you as his Queen. He sees you as the woman that he is in love with and the woman which he would give his life to protect. James just can't see himself, as only being a servant, to the Queen. He does not want to be your King or boss. He just wants to love you and, maybe someday, have you return that love.

Kieris looked down at the ground and smiled: Thank you for finding out for me. Now that I know, maybe I can get some sleep.

Archer smiled at her: That is what brothers are for. Sleep well, little sister. Archer leaves her tent. Kieris lies down and soon drifts off to sleep.

11: Training

Early the next morning, Kieris called everyone together. Kieris: We have a good plan together but while we are waiting for James to change you all to girls, we need to prepare. You men have had training, but your sons have not. I don't want to see anyone needlessly hurt, so just in case our plan doesn't go as smoothly as we would like; I want you to start training your sons to be able to at least protect themselves. Most of them will not be able to hold a sword, so start with bows and arrows, staffs and for the older boys maybe spears and swords. Find out what comes easier for them. Bowen, Archer, and I will come around and help with their training too.

Every day they all would gather together for breakfast and talk about the training they were planning to go over for the day. Then they broke up in four groups, one for each weapon. The groups would take lunch together and then continue training. They were not only teaching them how to use the weapons, but discipline and endurance. Kieris mainly helped with the bow and arrow training, Bowen mainly helped with the sword training, Archer mainly helped with the spear training and Robert the leader of the camp helped with the staff training. While they were doing that, James went around turning them all into women and girls. Every night they all would gather together for supper and talk about how the training went for that day.

Every three days the groups would rotate to a new weapon to try so they could find out where their strengths were. On Sunday there was no training, it was time for relaxing and spending time together. Kieris didn't want any of them to get burned out from training or the boys get frustrated with it. They were still children and needed some down time just to have a little fun and to be able to spend quality time with their dads. Those who wanted to train could but didn't have too.

During these Sundays; Kieris, Bowen, Archer and James would spend time together. Going over how their week had gone, what they thought of the boys' progress and just being together. James still hadn't gotten up the nerve to talk to Kieris about how he felt. The few times he tried, he was interrupted by one person or another and backed out. He would have to tell her soon, because it was driving him crazy not knowing how she felt. He figured that once he told her, he would be able to tell by her reaction, whether she said anything or not.

After two weeks of training the boys, the ones who just weren't able to handle any of the weapons safely or were no longer interested in learning were sent to James. James had already been given the weaker or smaller boys to help him. He was teaching them to act more like girls. Try to stay clean, not to play with bugs, to be scared of bugs and little things like that. Their voices hadn't changed yet for most of them, so they didn't need to practice on that much, except for a few things. They were not to talk about; hunting, fishing, fighting or anything else a girl wouldn't talk about. If they were not sure if it was something they could talk about, there were just to be quiet and act shy. These boys also helped James gather firewood, get water, set and check snares.

The other boys who had done well so far with the weapons were now getting advanced lessons in the weapon that they were doing the best with or the one they were more comfortable with if they had done well with more than one. Besides learning how to defend themselves with a large opponent, they also were learning how to work as a team. The boys would have three advantages over most men that would help them: one, they would look like girls and wouldn't be expected to know anything about fighting; two, they had more energy and stamina; and three, they were quicker than most men.

Kieris went to help James with his group of boys. Kieris: Boys, I have a special task I want you to do when we return. James and I are going to teach you a few tricks to protect yourselves and when we get back to the village, I need you to teach the girls these tricks when no one is watching. Can you do that for me? All of the boys were excited that they were still going to be able to help. Kieris: James, I hope you don't mind but I am going to tell two or three of the boys what I want them to try and they are going to try and trick you. Okay?

James laughed: Okay, but I get to tell them some tricks they can try on you too. Okay? Kieris laughed and shook her head yes.

Kieris gathered the boys around her so James wouldn't know how many were in on the trick. Then she asked James if he was ready. When he said yes; two of the boys acted like they were playing a game and got closer to him. They were just out of James's reach when all of a sudden, they ran at him and shoved him as hard as they could in the stomach and then ran. James fell backward over another boy that had snuck up behind him and was on his hands and knees next to the back of James's legs. That boy got up and ran too. All of the boys laughed because they liked that trick. James and Kieris laughed too.

James smiled: My turn.

Kieris: Okay, let's see what you got.

James gathered the boys around him and told them what he wanted them to do. James: Kieris, I am going to send one boy to you and you act like you're going to hurt him.

Kieris: Okay, whenever you're ready. Two boys came at her yelling and screaming to stop but stayed out of her reach. All of a sudden Kieris was being hit in the butt with little rocks, she let go of the boy she had hold of and turned around to see who was throwing things at her. It was two boys yelling for her to stop and then they ran off in two different directions. When she turned back around, the other three boys were gone.

Kieris: Very good. If there was someone that was hidden, and they were in danger of being found, you could use the first trick. If there was someone already in trouble, you would use the second trick. If a few of you were in trouble but still out of reach of the person, you would run as fast as you could in different directions. You are very smart boys. Tomorrow I want to see what you can come up with to go against two of us with the least amount of you doing it, and then I want to know in what situation you would use your trick. It's almost time for supper. Go wash up. James started to laugh when he caught Kieris rubbing her back side. Kieris laughed too but shook her finger at him at the same time.

The next day she had Bowen and Archer join them, because the boys asked for two big strong men to help with their trick. James and Kieris could not wait to see what the boys had come up with. One of the bigger boys in the group named Ricky stepped up to be their spokesperson. We need Bowen and Archer to each hold onto two boys, one boy in each hand, while we show you how we would get away. Kieris explained that they had been teaching the boys how to get out of different situation and this was something that they came up with on their own to show us what they have learned.

Bowen and Archer agreed and were a little curious at what they had been learning. Bowen and Archer got hold of the four boys who walked up to them. Kieris: Bowen and Archer, are you ready? They shook their heads yes. Kieris: Okay boys. You can begin. The boys they were holding started yelling, struggling, and kicking at Bowen and Archer but they held on tight to them. All of a sudden two boys with sticks came up behind them and hit Bowen and Archer in the back of the knees. Bowen and Archer let the other boys go so they could try to catch themselves, because the hits that they took made their knees buckle. The boys scattered and ran in different directions.

James, Kieris and the boys laughed. Bowen and Archer stood up. Bowen: Here we were worried about you boys but now I see you are very cunning and don't need special weapons. Archer: That is right; you worked very well together. That was a very good trick. You also have good teachers. They all laughed but Kieris and James wondered if they needed to be on guard for a trick to be pulled on them by

Bowen and Archer.

Kieris: I swear we had no idea what their trick was going to be. James: That is right; Kieris just told them to come up with a trick of their own. Kieris: We didn't know they would ask for two big strong men to help. We thought that whatever they came up with as a trick would be pulled on us. Bowen: Okay, we believe you. We won't do any tricks on either of you. Archer: Agreed, we won't do any tricks. Besides if we did then, your band of tricksters here might trick us back. They all laughed.

After Bowen and Archer left, Kieris and James told the boys how proud they were of them and how great they thought their trick was. Kieris: These and any other tricks you can think of are what I want you to teach the girls. You also need to find a safe place to hide until the danger is gone and you should always travel in groups of five or six. Making sure that at least three boys are with two or more girls at all times. They must not know that you are boys, so they will feel like they can do tricks too. When we are away at the castle, you boys will be in charge of teaching the girls more and more tricks and protecting them while we are away. This is a big job; do you think you can handle it? All of them were excited and said they could. Kieris smiled: That's great, now I want you to go help James while you think of some more tricks and I will check on you later.

The other boys were getting good enough with their weapons that they had started hunting with them, so they would have moving targets to aim at. Some of them were even good enough to shoot a rabbit on the run or spear a fish by throwing it from the bank. It had been almost three weeks and the boys were about as ready as they could be. Kieris just had to check with James to see if he had changed everyone's appearance so they would not be recognized. For now, they ate a good supper and went to bed. She would announce that they were leaving after she checked with James. He had acted like he wanted to talk to her a few times, but they would get interrupted. When she was done with whatever interrupted them, then he would be gone. The most time she had spent with him was when they were teaching the boys their tricks.

Early the next morning, while the rest of the camp was still asleep, James went to Kieris' tent. James: Kieris are you awake?

Kieris: Yes! Come in. James enters the tent and gets down on one knee, beside the bed that she is sitting on. James: I want to pledge my loyalty!

Kieris: Stop!

James: What is wrong?

Kieris: I don't want you to pledge anything, to

the Queen. I just want you to pledge your love to me!

James smiles at her: I pledge to you, the woman that I love, my heart, my protection and to always be there for you.

Kieris: I accept your pledge and in return, I pledge my love to you. (She smiled at him.) Have you turned all the Queen's soldiers, into women yet? They both laughed!

James: Yes! Your two brothers make a lovely pair of women, who look just like the Queen.

Kieris: Let's wake the camp, eat breakfast, and go back to the village to prepare the King's feast.

James: Just a minute! With your permission! He catches hold of her hands, pulls her up off the bed and onto her feet. Once on her feet, he wraps his arms around her waist and kisses her with all the passion he had in him. He had no experience and was scared to death he'd do it wrong.

James: You don't know how long I have wanted to do that! Now let's wake the camp.

Kieris stopped him: You don't know how long, I have waited for you, to do that. They kissed again. Kieris: Now as the Queen, let's wake the camp. They both laughed. As they were leaving Kieris tent, they met Archer and Bowen.

Bowen: I see you two have kissed and made up. Are you ready to get started?

James: Let's wake the camp and get them started.

Kieris: Yes! I am hungry! I am ready for breakfast and to get this over with!

Archer picked up a kettle and iron ladle and started banging them together: Rise and shine! Today is the day, that we free this land! Everyone get up! Boys, some of you get wood to build a fire and part of you get water to make coffee for the men. Soon the fire was going and the breakfast was nearly ready to eat. As they all sat down and ate, they went over their plans.

James: Remember your wives and daughters will not know who you are, so if you try to hug or kiss them, you may get your heads knocked off. They laughed. Boys remember they won't see you as their sons and brothers either. Practice talking with a female voice, as we move toward the village. No one must know what we are up to or this plan will fail. We will hunt along the way so there is meat enough to feed your families and to cook for the King's big feast.

Kieris: Bowen and Archer, you must keep your

faces covered at all times. Three of me would confuse the people and put the King on guard. Making them look like me now, may have been a bad idea.

James: I will fix that! He chanted a spell and Bowen and Archer no longer looked like Kieris. I will change them back to look like Kieris when we enter the palace with our feast and wedding gifts.

Archer: Remember your Queen has given the order that the King is not to be harmed. He is to be captured and put on trial for his crimes against his people.

Bowen: His top guards are also to be captured and tried for their crimes.

Kieris: We are going to try out best to capture them all so no one gets hurt. Justice, honest and fair treatment, for all the people of this land, guilty or not!

When breakfast was over, they broke camp and headed for the village. Along the way to the village, the men hunted; killing animals for the feast, and for the villagers. By the time they had gotten to the village, they had killed one large grizzly bear, four large buck deer, six wild turkeys, and four large wild boar hogs. They had also killed a dozen each of squirrels, rabbits, ground hogs and pheasants. The whole village would eat tonight, and they would still have a large variety of meats left over for the feast. The King would think that the feast was for his wedding, but it would really be to celebrate the end of his reign of terror.

12: Freedom

When they got to the village they were met by six armed guards. Guard one: Halt! What are you doing? Why did you come here and where did you get all that meat?

Kieris: We have gathered this meat to prepare a great feast for our King and his new bride.

Guard: What new bride?

Kieris: Have you not heard? He is going to be married, to our Princes Kieris! Kieris has agreed to marry him to bring peace back to this land. Send runners to all the villages to join us. Let the King know of this feast. We will be bringing all this food, wedding gifts, and his bride to the palace for the wedding in two days. Now hurry spread the word. We celebrate our freedom and the King's wedding in two days.

Word was sent to the King. The King ordered the great arena prepared for the feast and wedding so everyone in the Kingdom could attend. They fixed a small amount of the meat and fed the village that night. The next day was spent preparing all the meat that they had killed, as well as gathering apples, peaches, pears, and grapes from the nearby orchards. They also gathered roses, pansies, poppies, and wild flowers from the fields to be used as decorations at the feast. Many trips were made taking everything, except for the cooked food, to the arena and setting everything up for the grand feast. The King did not trust anyone, so all the women were searched for weapons. The armory in the palace was full of weapons, so they did not have to try and sneak any weapons in from the outside. The guards stopped Bowen at the gate because he was the first one to reach the gate with food and the rest were following him. Guard: Where is Princess Kieris? Bowen answered in a voice as much like a woman as he could manage: Well sweetie! The princess will arrive in the morning, in time for the wedding along with all the cooked food for the feast. We will watch the wedding and then we will all feast. We will eat, drink and dance, it is going to be a party like none ever before.

Bowen took his hand and touched the guards face. I will save you the first dance, good looking. He then picked back up the bushel of apples, which he had set down and went on into the palace grounds. He was followed closely by all the other men carrying food, baskets of fruit and baskets of flowers but all the guards could see was a lot of women. The guard told the King what he had been told about when Princess Kieris would arrive. Guard: I was told that princess Kieris would arrive at ten a.m. and the wedding will take place at once. Then everyone will feast; celebrating the wedding and the crowning of our new Queen. While the guards had gone to tell the King, some of the men had sneaked into the palace armory, getting weapons, and hiding them in and around the arena, so they would have them to use tomorrow. The guards did not notice that they had left for a while, because some of the other men, which they saw as women, had flirted with them to keep their attention. Once they had finished decorating, hiding the weapons, and putting the baskets of fruit on tables that had been set up in the arena, they left.

The King stood on the balcony outside his room early the next morning, he watched for the arrival of the crowd and his new Queen to be. He was waiting for the arrival of the princess. At ten a.m. sharp, a coach being pulled by six white horses entered through the palace gates. The coach was driven by Robert, the leader from the camp of the King's deserted guards; but what the guards at the palace and all the others there could see was the coach was being driven by a woman. Robert: Behold, I have brought the Princess Kieris and her maidens in waiting. The coach contained Bowen and Archer, who now looked like the princess Kieris. James and Kieris were also in the coach, now dressed and looking like her maidens in waiting. The princess asked to talk to the King alone before the wedding. The King who had been watching from the small upstairs balcony agreed. Everyone in the coach got out and entered the palace.

They all went to the throne room. Once inside,

the King asked to see Kieris' face. Bowen uncovered his face. King: My princess! Today you will become my Queen. Guards you are dismissed! Kieris send your maids away, so we can talk alone. The guards left followed by Kieris and James. That left Bowen who looked like Kieris to face him. Archer stayed, hidden behind one of the large hanging wall rugs. Bowen slowly moved to the Kings left and a little closer to where he was standing. He had the King's attention.

Archer moved over and looked out the throne room door to make sure that the guards had gone. He then moved to the right of where the King was standing and closer to him. King: Stop! What is this? The King drew his sword.

Bowen: Would you kill your Queen to be?

King: No but I would kill her! Archer uncovered his face, so that the King could see that he too could also be Kieris.

Archer: We are not here to harm you.

Bowen: We are here to help. By then the King had sat down, too confused to do anything.

Bowen and Archer quickly disarmed the King and let James and Kieris back into the throne room. Kieris went out on the balcony, which overlooked the arena to talk to the people. Kieris: People the King has been captured. The land is now free! While she was talking, the men had captured the guards and James had turned the men back so everyone could see them, for who they were. This land is now free; all that is left for you, the people, to do; is crown a new ruler. The men that had helped her started yelling. Long live Queen Kieris. The second time they started to yell it; the people joined in and were also calling for Kieris to be their Queen.

Kieris held up her hands to gain silence: If you want me to be your Queen, then I accept. After I am crowned, we will hold trials for the King and all his guards which helped him. She went back inside. They had captured the King and all his guards. They had saved the land, without killing anyone. Bowen and Archer were proud, of what they had done. They had found the Chosen One. They had helped the people of this land, to free themselves from the cruel King, without having to kill anyone. They had found and saved their long-lost sister, which they didn't even know that they had. Tomorrow would be the trial of the King and his evil followers. The people had accepted the fact that the King and his men would be tried for their crimes; but the people were in for a surprise!

The next morning, the princess had all the prisoners taken to the arena for the trials to begin. The arena stands were already filled with the people. Kieris: People, we are here to try these prisoners for their crimes against humanity. I will be the judge over this trial and you, the people of this land, will be the jury. You will decide if they are guilty or not, but it will be my job to sentence them for these crimes, if you find them guilty.

The people started yelling: Guilty! Guilty! Guilty!

Kieris held up her hands for silence: This will not do! You have not heard the charges against them. You have not heard the evidence against them. You have not taken into account, why they did these things. You have to hear, see and then decide; if they are guilty.

Would you find a six-year-old boy guilty if he stole an apple from the store only to find out later that he stole it not for himself but for a younger two-year-old sister who was starving to death? Would you sentence him to death for stealing, or because he did it to save a life, only make him work to pay for the food? Now think about these two children, as being your children. Justice must be fair to all people. When needed, there must be mercy in the sentencing. If you are not willing to be fair and just to everyone guilty or not, then you need to find someone else to be your ruler. I will not be the kind of ruler that the King was; or our fight to free this land will have been in vain.

Bowen: You know that what she says is

true. Look at your own lives! Are you not guilty of doing something which was against the King's laws? Didn't some of you take in your neighbors that had no home and hide the fact, so you could afford to pay the taxes to keep your homes? Didn't some of you feed people, when the King had said let them starve? You hid people to keep the King's guards from killing them, because they had not really done anything wrong. Should you be punished for that under the King's law, you broke the law; or should we find out why you did it, and then decide how guilty you are!

Archer: We are not from this country, but we have fought to help free you, so that you could live in peace. Live in a fair and just land, where you have choices. Where you are not told what you can do for a living or where you can work. Live in a land, where you can choose to live in peace. Freedom to live in a land, where the ruler tries to help the people, not make them his or her slaves! Decide now what you want! Are we having a trial, or are you hunting for a new slave driver to rule you? The crowd was silent, looking back and forth at each other. One of the guards, who had helped free the land, dropped to one knee, lowered his head, and began to yell. Guard: The King is no more our ruler. Long live Queen Kieris!

He kept repeating, what he had said. The other guards and their families, who had helped free the land, joined him yelling the same thing.

Soon, everyone in the arena had joined them yelling. The King is no longer our ruler, long live Queen Kieris. Kieris held up her hands for silence. Everyone stopped yelling and there was silence in the arena. Kieris motioned for the guards to bring a statue of a woman holding a scale in her hands into the arena. The statue had long been a symbol, of fair weights and measures, for the crops produced and sold in this land. A scarf had been added to the statue and it covered the statue's eyes, so that the woman holding the scales could not see.

Kieris: This is our new symbol for justice! People will be tried for the crimes that they have done and using the evidence that we have against them. Not based on who they are, what they own and who or what that they can buy. The decree of guilty or not must be based on the facts, not on who they are! Not on the person themselves. Today we will try these people, on what they did and why. We will find them guilty or not! I am princess Kieris and as such, I cannot sentence them. Tomorrow you will crown a new ruler, be it me or someone else. Your new ruler will sentence the guilty for their crimes and pardon the ones which you find not guilty.

Not guilty because of why they broke the King's law! So, these first trials will be fair to the prisoners, none of you will know who you are trying; just what their crimes were and why they did these crimes. After each verdict is rendered, you will be told who you found guilty or innocent. All the prisoners will be returned to their cells until time to sentence them. There will be two men giving you the facts, in each of these cases. One of these men will be trying to get you to find the person guilty and one of these men will be telling you why you should find them innocent. Then you will decide. These men don't know who they are defending or trying to convict either. It could be your own brothers, sisters, wives, or others who are related to you or them. That way, justice will be fair, just like the blind statue with the scales. We will call these men lawyers. For they will be working for this land, its laws, and to punish the guilty and set the innocent free! So there can be justice for everyone.

Kieris had asked Bowen and Archer, to take care of the trials for her. The trials were held by only giving a number to each person on trial. Only Bowen and Archer would know what number belonged to which prisoner. Kieris could not pass out the punishment, for the ones that the people found guilty, until after she had been crowned Queen. The boys would see that the trials were conducted fairly. They then made a list, of who the people had found guilty and who they thought should be pardoned. The people had even given recommendations of mercy with some of the guilty findings.

Kieris returned to the palace to try and get some rest. She went into the throne room and sat down in the King's chair. Not much had changed since she had run away. They had only changed the color of the curtains over the windows and the color of the table cloth on the long table in front of the throne. This was the table where the King would sit and hold his meetings, with all the noblemen. He would sit at the head of the table. She sat there looking out across the long table and remembered hiding in the secret room; watching the King and hearing him give things to the noblemen, which belonged to the poor of this land.

She was sure that they would try to keep her from becoming Queen. They knew that she thought what the King did was unfair to the poor. She did not have any of the noblemen arrested to be tried for their crimes; but knew that she would have to deal with them if she became Queen. She heard some men coming down the hall, toward the throne room. She did not know who they were, so she opened the door into the secret hidden room and went inside. When they entered the throne room she could hear them talking, it was four of the noblemen that used to visit the King. The King had used this room, to spy on everyone in the throne room and listen to them talk about him.

The Earl of Kent entered the room first: She is not here! She has to be in the palace somewhere, she is not at the trials.

Next to enter the room is the Earl of Mobile: We can't let her become the Queen. We will have to find a way to get rid of her, even if we have to kill her.

The third nobleman, the Earl of Carnes enters the room: We better come up with someone to offer the people to take her place as the ruler of this land.

The last nobleman enters; he is the Earl of Cowan: You're right! We can't let her become Queen and we do need someone to become the new ruler. Maybe Merlin can help us with these problems. Let's go talk to him. Then all four of them left the throne room and headed toward the prisoner's cells.

James had gone to get Kieris something to eat and drink. He saw the noblemen leave the throne room and hurried into the room, to make sure that Kieris was all right. She was standing next to the throne, when he entered the room. James: Are you all right? I saw the noblemen leave.

Kieris: I am ok. They did not see me! They are going to see if Merlin can help them stop me from becoming Queen.

James: Stay here out of sight; I will take care of this. I will be back! James leaves the food and drinks then hurries toward the prison. By the time the noblemen get to Merlin's cell,

James has already had him moved.

He has made himself to look like Merlin and had taken Merlin's place in the cell. Kieris took the food and drink back into the secret room, to hide and wait on James. After eating, she lay down and fell fast asleep. Earl of Kent: Merlin! Merlin! Wake up! Merlin do you know what has happened?

James: Yes. I, Merlin, am being tried for my crimes.

Earl of Carnes: No! We mean have you heard about the people wanting to make the princess Kieris their Queen?

Earl of Cowan: If she becomes Queen, she could ruin us all.

Earl of Mobile: Merlin can you help us? Will you help us?

James: She is young and won't know what to do as a Queen. She had everyone arrested for their crimes; but she did not have any of you arrested.   What are you worried about? You did not take the lands you own from the poor. The King gave them to you as gifts. It would not be just or fair to take your lands back away from you.

Earl of Kent: He is right! She is new and maybe if we seem to support her we can become her advisors and use her.

Earl of Carnes: Merlin can we count on you to help us?

James: As surely as you are standing there looking at Merlin, I will help do what is best for us all. Once these trials are over, I will try to get the new Queen to call a meeting of all the noblemen to help advise her. That is if the people don't find Merlin guilty and the Queen doesn't have him put to death. Now leave me!

The noblemen leave the prison going back to their own homes. James changes back, so he looks like himself, returns Merlin to his cell and then returns to the throne room, but finds no one there. Since Kieris was no place to be seen, he returns to the arena to see if she went back to the trials. The last trial had ended, just as James got there. The list was made of who was guilty and who was not. They would just have to wait for Kieris to become Queen tomorrow, before they could proceed with the sentencing. Kieris was not there either. James told Bowen and Archer, what had happened with the noblemen. They all three returned to the palace to find Kieris.

13: Kieris' Hidden Room

They entered the throne room but saw no one.
Bowen: Let's look around to see if she left a
note or something, which might tell us where
she went.

Archer: It doesn't look like she was taken by
force.

James: By force?

Archer laughed: If someone had taken her, she
would have broken a few things!

Bowen: Yes, she is a fighter! The noise of them
searching and talking had awakened Kieris.
The throne slid away from the wall revealing
the secret door and Kieris walked out into the
throne room, where the others were standing.

James: That is a neat trick! A hidden room!

Kieris: The King's private spying room. He
doesn't even know that I know about the secret
room or how to get into it.

James: Let's keep it a secret! Was Merlin found
guilty at the trials?

Bowen: Yes. Because he helped us find Kieris,
he was granted mercy by the people! So, it
depends on whatever sentence Kieris gives
him.

Archer: I will post guards outside Kieris' royal rooms and this throne room. Kieris you can sleep in the hidden room and we will sleep out here. Everyone will think that you are in your own room and that will make it easier for us to protect you. Go back into your hidden room until I get beds in here for us and some food for all of us to eat.

Kieris: Ok. She went back into the secret room and closed the door. Archer went to Kieris' royal rooms with a group of guards. Archer: Guard these rooms and your new Queen. Let no one enter her rooms except James, Bowen, or me. She needs some rest; tomorrow will be a busy day for her. I am holding you all responsible for her safety. He then instructed the maids to bring bedding and food to the throne room. He also posted two guards outside the throne room, after the bedding and food had been delivered. When everyone else was gone, except for the three of them, Bowen locked the throne room door from the inside. Kieris came back out of the hidden room and they all sat down at the long wooden table to eat.

James: You know, I like a round table; that way you can all see each other.

Kieris: That would make it easier to talk to each other. When they finished eating, Kieris went back into the secret room and went to bed for the night. The boys also turned in for the night.

They were awakened early the next morning by a guard beating on the throne room door. James unlocked the door and opened it: What is wrong?

Guard: The two guards which were posted outside the princess' door have been killed and the princess is missing.

Bowen: Wait for us out in the hall! The guard went back outside the throne room and waited. Archer closed and locked the door behind him. James opened the secret door to check on Kieris. Kieris was still asleep.

James woke her and told her what had happened. James: Here is my sword. Stay hidden, we will return.

Kieris: Don't worry. I can lock the secret door from inside, so it can't be opened from the outside. (She kissed him.) Be careful!

James: I will be right back, and I will be careful. He hugged her and gave her an ardent kiss before he left the room. She closed and locked the door behind him.

Bowen: Is everything all right with Kieris?

James: Yes. Let's go find out who broke into

Kieris' room and who killed the guards.

Archer: We need to let the guards hunt for Kieris too. The boys gathered all the guards. The ones they weren't sure was loyal to Kieris, they sent to search for her; the ones they knew were loyal to Kieris, they had them search the palace for anyone who did not belong there. They removed everyone from the palace who did not belong there and closed the gates; so, no one else could enter or leave the palace. The guards were turning everyone away from the palace gates. The noblemen were upset that they were not let into the palace and demanded to see the princess. Archer talked to the noblemen from the top of the wall around the palace. Archer: Noblemen! I am here to tell the noblemen that the princess wants them all to attend a meeting in the throne room tomorrow. She also wants the Bishop to be there to crown her as the new Queen. The noblemen looked at each other without saying a word then left.

Bowen: They sure did not look happy!

James: They did look surprised that the princess was still alive enough to give orders.

Archer: Yes, they did look surprised.

Guard: We don't know where the princess is or if she is ok!

Bowen: Yes, and now we know that they don't know either.

Guard: I see, they were trying to find out if the ones who broke into her room had killed her or not. Now they will think that she is alive. We did not catch the ones who broke into her room. They have not been able to let the noblemen know if they were able to kill her or not. That means that the ones who did this and killed the guards are still in the palace.

Archer: Right! James, go back to the throne room, lock the door behind you so you're locked in and wait for us. Bowen and I will search the palace for the princess and the ones who broke into her room and killed the guards. Lock yourself in the throne room and guard it. James returned to the throne room, made sure that it was empty and then locked himself in the room. Once the room was locked and safe, he called for Kieris to unlock the secret room door, so he could make sure that she was all right. She came out into the throne room.

Kieris: James, I am scared! He took her into his arms holding her close.

James: Don't worry! I will not let anything happen to you. Your brothers are searching the palace now, for the men who broke into your room.

Kieris: I don't want to be Queen! I just want us

all to be safe.

James: There! There! Everything is going to be ok. (James kissed her.) Your brothers and I will always be here for you, Queen or not. There is a knock on the throne room door. Kieris quickly returned to the secret room and locked herself inside. James walked over near the door, so he could hear: Who is there?

Bishop: It is I, the Bishop! James unlocked the door and opened it. He wondered how the Bishop had gotten into the palace, as everyone was being turned away at the gate.

James: Your lordship, what can I do for you?

Bishop: I thought that the princess might be in here.

James: No. There is no one here in the throne room but me.

The Bishop walked into the room and looked around, until he was sure that only the two of them were in the room. Bishop: I heard that she wanted to talk to me.

James: No, she doesn't. I would like to ask you a few questions, if I may. What if Kieris decides that she doesn't want to be the Queen?

Bishop: If Kieris does not become Queen then the noblemen would pick the new ruler.

James: You mean the people would not have any say in who would become the new ruler?

Bishop: That is right, only the well-educated would be able to choose and that would be the noblemen.

James: Could Kieris appoint a new ruler?

Bishop: As princess she could not appoint a new ruler, but as Queen she could.

James: Thank you, your lordship, for the information. We need you here by noon tomorrow; which is when Princess Kieris wanted to see you along with all the noblemen, so a new ruler can be crowned.

Bishop: I will be here, my son. The Bishop left the room; James closed and locked the door behind him.

The Bishop left the palace and went straight to the Earl of Kent's castle, where all the noblemen were waiting for him.

Earl of Kent: Well, what did you find out, is she dead?

Bishop: I did not see the princess anywhere, but by the questions that they were asking me, I would say that she is either dead or has run away again. Either way, she doesn't want to be Queen!

Earl of Carnes: That is great news! Now we need to pick someone to become the new ruler!

Bishop: Yes. Tomorrow we must crown a new ruler, one way or another. Back in the palace, Bowen and Archer had found the men who had killed the guards and broke into Kieris' room. The problem was; they had all been killed before the boys were able to question them, to find out who had hired them.

The palace was now secured, being guarded only by the guards that were loyal to Kieris and had helped her fight to free this land. The other guards were sent outside the palace, to patrol and keep a look out for anyone trying to sneak in. They weren't sure about them but didn't want to offend them either. The boys told the guards that Kieris was safe, that the wizard was hiding her and then they returned to the throne room. Bowen and Archer brought food, water, and the prettiest dress that they could find in Kieris' room, for her to wear to become Queen. They also brought things, so she could bathe before she dressed to meet with them to be crowned. She would want to look her best to become Queen. Once everything was in the throne room, the door was closed and locked from the inside. Kieris unlocked the secret room door and joined them in the throne room. She looked very sad and upset.

Archer: Kieris, what is wrong?
Bowen: Yes, little sister, what is bothering you now?

James: I don't think that she wants to be Queen.

Kieris: No, I don't want to be Queen! I don't have any choice! We didn't fight to free this land, to let the evil noblemen run it like the King did. The Bishop was here, and James questioned him to find out what would happen if I turned down the job as Queen.

Archer: How did he get into the palace?

James: I don't know but I wondered that myself. No one saw the men that killed the guards enter the palace either.

Bowen: There has to be another way into the palace, besides the main gate.

Archer: Kieris none of us wanted this fight or the jobs that we have now. If you become Queen, we will help you in any way we can.

Bowen: Because you become Queen, doesn't mean that you have to remain Queen forever!

James: That is right! You can become Queen, we can finish cleaning up this land and then you can appoint your own replacement. That is, if you decide then, that you no longer want to be Queen.

Kieris smiled: That sounds like something that I can live with, at least for now. The boys moved her bath and clothes into the secret room. She went into the room and closed the door. While she bathed and changed into her night clothes, the boys fixed something to eat.

James: We are going to have to find out, how they got in and put a stop to them entering that way or Kieris will not be safe, even after she becomes Queen.

Bowen: I will have the guards and staff hunting for a secret passage. There has to be one; for that would be the only way someone could get in without being seen. Kieris returned to the throne room, dressed in her night clothes. They all sat down and ate. They would all go to bed early that night, for tomorrow would be a long hard day for them all. Kieris slept in her secret room, with the door locked from the inside.

The next morning while everyone else slept, James hung blankets across the back of the room, so he could use them like curtains to hide the throne. That way, he could make it look like he made Kieris appear and still protect her secret hiding place. A guard beats on the throne room door. Bowen wakes up and answers the door. Bowen: What do you want?

Guard: The noblemen and Bishop are at the gate, wanting to come into the palace.

Archer: Let the noblemen and the Bishop in, but don't let their guards or anyone else who is with them, come into the palace. Take them all to the library to wait. Tell them we are fixing the throne room and getting it ready for the crowning of the new ruler.

Guard: Yes, sir! The guard leaves. Bowen closes and locks the door.

James opened the blankets like curtains, to reveal the thrown. He beat on the wall to wake Kieris. Kieris unlocks and opens the room door. James: Good morning! Did you sleep well?

Kieris: Yes! Knowing that the job of Queen will only be temporary, helped me sleep a lot better.

Bowen: Are you ready to become Queen? The people are already gathered under the window balcony, to greet the new ruler of this land and are waiting to see their new Queen.

Archer: Kieris, we need you to make the noblemen think that they will be your new advisors, once you become Queen. That will make it easier for you to become Queen. Kieris smiled: I have been thinking about that and I know just how to do it. While Kieris dressed for her crowning, the boys cleared the throne room and set the large long table back in place. They placed wine and wine glasses on the table. Finally, everything was ready.

Kieris: I will see the noblemen first, then the Bishop comes in and crown me. She sat down on the thrown and James drew the curtains to hide her.

Bowen opened the door. Bowen: Guards bring in just the noblemen and seat them. The noblemen were brought into the throne room and seated at the table. Wine was poured into each glass.

Earl of Kent: Where is the princess? Where is princess Kieris?

James: Here! He opened the curtains to reveal Kieris sitting on the thrown. The noblemen all stood.

Kieris: Please be seated! The King reserved these seats for his trusted advisors. I will do the same. Will you all do your best to help me run this country? Will you all be available to serve me as your Queen, if I need you to advise me as you advised and helped the King?

The noblemen were surprised! Had Kieris just asked them to be her advisors and help her run this land? It was more than they could have hoped for. They would have to call off the men that they had hired to kill her. They would let her be crowned Queen, because now it looked like, they would still be able to be in charge of running the country. Earl of Carnes: Princess will you be letting your brothers and wizard help to advise you?

Kieris: No. They are in charge of my security and the security of the palace. The noblemen all stood up and held up their glasses of wine. The King is no more! Long live princess Kieris! Long live Queen Kieris! Kieris is handed a glass of wine by James. She raises her glass and makes a toast: To my trusted advisors, who will sit in these seats, advise me, and who will help me run this country. They all raised their glasses and took a drink.

Earl of Mobile: Excuse us princess! We have a few things to do, before you are crowned. When will you meet with your advisors?

Kieris: I will be letting them know, when and where we will meet. Before the meeting with them, I will have to sentence all of the prisoners, which have been found guilty. I will need your help soon. The noblemen left the throne room. James made sure that they were gone: Well played! You did not ask or tell them that they would be your advisors but let them think that they would be.

Kieris: I want to see all the guards that helped us free this land. The ones from the camp!

James: Ok. But it needs to be a secret meeting!

Kieris: Not really! Everyone will think that I am making safety arrangements for the crowning of the Queen.

Archer, Bowen and James gathered all of Kieris' trusted guards into the throne room, so she could talk to them. Kieris: Please be seated! They all sat down. I want each of you to find someone in your village, which will represent those people and the village's best interest, not their own interest and greed. I want to meet with them here in the throne room tomorrow morning. They are to tell no one that I sent for them or why they are coming to the castle. If asked, they came to swear loyalty to the new Queen. A guard held up his hand to ask a question.

Kieris: Yes, you may speak. What is your question? Guard: Can we ask why you want to talk to them? It would help us pick the best person to help you, with whatever you want to see them for.

Kieris: Yes, I will tell you why I want to see them, but you can't tell anyone why, not even them. I need to appoint some advisors to help me. Who better to know what the village needs, than someone from that village? Not all problems will be solved, but it will help me make changes that will help the most people. The guards left. Two hours later, the noblemen had contacted the ones that they had hired to kill her. The noblemen were now on their way back to the castle, so the Bishop could crown the new Queen.

14: Queen Kieris

The nuns from the nearby church had helped Kieris get ready in her suite of rooms for her crowning. Nun: Your Highness, the Queen had given this to me to keep safe. She showed Kieris a beautiful wooden carved jewelry box. She handed it to Kieris. Nun: The Queen said that she would retrieve it from me and give it to you, on your wedding day or when you became Queen. Kieris looked at the box closely. It was made out of cherry wood with a glossy finish. The carvings on the lid of the box looked like a picture of the Queen and a younger Kieris bow shooting. Around the side was the scenery and village they would walk to, to visit the most and the orchard they had picked fruit from to give to the villagers. There was paint in the carvings to make them stand out more before it was sealed by the gloss.

With tears in her eyes she looked at the nun. Kieris: Thank you. This means a lot to me.

Nun: That is not all, look inside. Kieris opened the box; the inside was lined with red silk and in the bottom of the box was a gold necklace with a gold locket on it. On the top of the locket was etched an apple with an arrow through it. Inside was a picture of the Queen and on the inside lid were the words; To Thine Own Self Be True. This time Kieris could not keep from crying, she grabbed the nun and hugged her.

Kieris: Thank you for keeping this safe. I will never forget this. If there is anything that you ever need, please let me know.

Nun smiled at Kieris: God provides me with what I need. I was just doing what the Queen asked of me. Seeing your reaction to the Queen's gift is all the thanks I need for doing my duty. The nun helped Kieris put the necklace on.

She finished getting ready, put the jewelry box away in a cloth bag to take to the safe room in the throne room and composed herself some. She gave the nun another hug and then tucked the necklace inside the top of her dress so it would be near her heart. When the nuns left her bedroom, Bowen and Archer then sneaked her back into the throne room. Archer told Kieris, that James wanted her to hide behind the curtains, which he had hung in front of the thrown. The noblemen and Bishop were brought into the room and seated. James had not seen her yet and when the curtain was opened, she was so beautiful standing there, that it made James, catch his breath.

She stood there in a long white dress, with the royal robes around her shoulders. She held the Bible in one hand and the royal scepter in the other. Her hair framed her face in long flowing curls. Kieris was indeed the most beautiful woman any of them had ever seen. The noblemen and Bishop all stood to their feet.

The nuns had entered the room for the crowning. The Bishop moved over to the closest nun that was holding the new crown, which had been made just for the new Queen. He took the crown and moved over to Kieris, so he could put it on her head.

Bishop: Princes Kieris do you swear to serve the people of this land. Obey God's laws. To help and protect the people of this land, rich and poor alike.

Kieris: I swear to help and protect the people of this land, from those outside and inside this country, who would harm them.

The Bishop put the crown on Kieris' head. Bishop: I now crown you Queen Kieris. You are now the Queen of all these people and all the lands that belong to this country. Everyone smiled and raised their glasses of wine: Long live Queen Kieris! She smiled, walked out on the balcony, and waved to all the people below. They were all yelling: Long live, the Queen! She went back inside.

Kieris: It has been a long day and I am tired. Tomorrow, we will have the swearing of loyalty. Tonight, all I want to do is get some rest. Wizard James, if you don't mind, to my room please. She sat down on the throne and James drew the curtain in front of her. She entered the secret room and locked the door, as he mumbled, as if transporting her into the royal suites. He reopened the curtains, so that they could see that she was gone.

The noblemen and Bishop left while James, Bowen and Archer cleaned up the throne room. Tomorrow would be a busy day, for everyone in the country would be lined up to pledge their loyalty to the Queen. Her brothers Bowen and Archer along with James and all the palace guards had already pledged their loyalty to her. She had James create a round table and she had knighted the guards, giving them the right to correct any wrongs, which they saw being done to the poor of the land.

The next morning, Kieris was sitting on the throne, as they started letting people in to see the Queen. The noblemen were the first in line to pledge their loyalty to her. Each of them brought her a gift, as they pledged their loyalty. One gave her a fur coat, to keep her warm in the winter. Another one gave to her, a golden bath tub to bathe in. One gave her, a beautiful black stallion to ride. One gave her, a carriage and six white horses to pull it. One of the noblemen had even given her, a gold and diamond necklace, tiara, and earrings to match. The Bishop gave her, a necklace of gold with pearl prayer beads. Her servants took the gifts, as they were given and placed them in her room, that is all except the carriage and horses, which were taken to the stables. The noblemen and the Bishop left. It was now the common people that she loved so much, coming into pledge their loyalty to their new Queen. They brought her gifts too; of food, flowers, and handmade pieces of clothes. These were the gifts that she cherished the most.

She was thinking ahead about the advisors and sentencing the prisoners. When everyone had left, she sent word to the men that the guards had picked from each village, the noblemen and the Bishop, that she wanted to meet with them the next afternoon because it was time to seat her advisors. So, the noblemen could not corrupt her panel of advisors, she had James to help her write up a list of what the advisors could and could not do. That the final decision would always be hers. They could not over rule her decisions. Being Queen was hard work and she had not had much time to spend with James and her brothers. She was so tired that she slept soundly, hidden in the secret room.

The next morning, she was awakened by a knock on the secret door. Not sure who it was, she waited for them to call out her name, so she would know that it was not, just someone cleaning the throne room. James: Kieris! Kieris! She unlocked the door and James entered the room, carrying a tray of food. She locked the door behind him. James: I brought you some breakfast.

Kieris: Thank you.

James: I was hoping that we could spend at least a few minutes together.

Kieris: I would like that. Sorry that we can't spend more time together right now. This job as Queen is taking up all my time and I hate it. I am hoping that after I get the advisors seated and these trials over, I will have more time to do what I want to do.

James: What are you going to do, about the noblemen?

Kieris: I will appoint the village men to collect and bring me the complaints of the people. Have them come up with ways, that they think these problems can be solved. Let them sit in on all the advisor meetings, so they can see what the noblemen have to say about these problems and how to solve them. Then they will know the truth about the noblemen and what they are doing for themselves and can tell the villages what is really happening, so the noblemen can't change it and try to blame me. This will force the noblemen to at least try to solve some of the problems. My new knights will visit the villages, to make sure the laws are being enforced.

James: They will still blame you, since you have the last word on every matter.

Kieris: Not if it is made into a law right then and there, at the meeting. Then there is no way, the nobleman can change it to put the blame on me, because these village men will know what the real and true laws are.

James: Smart! Kieris sat and ate her breakfast as James told her what her brothers had been doing. Bowen and Archer had been talking to people and finding new guards that they could trust, to guard the palace and her. They had also remodeled the royal suites, to make them a safer place, so she could move back into them. While remodeling the royal suites, they had also included a hidden safety room there too. As Kieris finished her breakfast, they could hear Bowen and Archer in the throne room talking.

They waited to make sure that they were alone before they left the safety of the hidden room. Bowen: James! Kieris! It is safe to come out now. James and Kieris joined Bowen and Archer, in the main throne room.

Kieris: What is going on now?

Archer: It is almost time for the nobles and men from the village to arrive, so you can seat your advisors.

Kieris: Ok! I will be back in a few minutes. I will have to go dress for the meeting. Seat them all in the library, that way there is enough seats for them all to sit down. She left the room.

James: I will wait on her and bring her to the library, when she is ready.

Bowen and Archer were already being called to the gates as people were arriving for the advisors meeting. The noblemen were at the gate waiting. They wondered, why there were villagers there too. Archer and Bowen took them all to the library, seating the noblemen on the first level, at the large oval table that had been taken from the throne room. They seated the villagers in the chairs on the second level, where they could see all the noblemen. The noblemen sat whispering to each other, while they waited on the Queen to arrive. Kieris entered the room and they all stood. She moved to the chair that had been placed at one side of the large table, away from where the noblemen were seated and sat down. Kieris: Please, everyone sit down! Everyone sat down.

I am new at being a Queen, so I have asked for help. Noblemen you will help me solve the problems which we have in this country. To do that, we have to know what the problems are, that we face. I have asked the villages to send one person, with a list of what they feel needs to be done and how they think that we may be able to fix the problems. Noblemen, you will help me decide which problems that we can fix and the best way to do it. You have all been given the list of rules for advisors. You can only suggest ways to fix or change things, the final decision is mine. Villagers, you have to understand, that not all the problems can be fixed at once. It will take time to fix the ones that we can; and some problems we may never be able to fix.

Noblemen you have to understand that by helping solve the country's problems, it will make the country safer, produce more and increase the wealth of the poor and rich alike. Villagers give your lists of things that need fixed and your suggestion for fixing them to James. He will make copies of them for me and all the noblemen. The noblemen will take their copies with them, so they can come up with ways to fix these problems. We will meet back here in one week, to discuss the problems and possible solutions. Kieris got up and left the room, before anyone could ask her any questions.

James collected the papers from the villagers, while the noblemen sat whispering among themselves. All the villagers left the castle.

Earl of Carnes: James would you ask the Queen to join us, we have some questions that we need answers to, before we can work on these lists.

James: Ok, wait here, I will see if she will come back and talk to you. While James was gone, they talked about the list.

Earl of Kent: We can't meet these demands; it would cost us a fortune.

Earl of Mobile: I wonder just what this new Queen has in mind! We can't afford to do these things and we can't afford to offend the Queen.

James reentered the room: Queen Kieris will be here in a minute, to talk with you. They all sat quietly and waited for her to return to the room. Kieris entered, accompanied by her brothers, Bowen and Archer. They all stood until after she had been seated and she told them to sit back down. Kieris: Gentlemen I know that you are confused. In order to stabilize this country, we must all work together rich and poor alike. The poor will not work with us if they don't see any changes being made that will help them. We can't afford to fix everything on their lists.

We must find a way to fix the cheapest things, so that we can give them hope and so they can start to see things getting better for them. Right now you receive 90% of the crops that are raised on your lands and the poor receive only 10%. If we cut into your profits by another 10%, we can do a lot of changes that will help them and still help us too.

Earl of Kent: We can't afford that!

Kieris: Yes you can, and still not lose a penny.

Earl of Carnes: How?

Kieris: Right now you raise 10 acres of crops on each of your properties, with the village people doing all the work and you each receive 100 dollars per acre, of that you pay the villagers 10 per each acre. You pay the crown another 40, which leaves you 50 per acre profit.

Earl of Carnes: That is right!

Kieris: What if you increase your crops by one acre each. The villagers are still doing all the work. That acre is worth 100 dollars. That is what you are paying the villagers for the 10 acres now, so that would mean that you were getting the 10 acres raised for free. Then from the extra acre, your taxes to the crown would go up by 40 dollars and that is the money that would be used, to make the changes and fix some of the things on the villager's lists. That would make your profits go up from fifty percent to sixty percent and your crops worked for free. They know that everything can't be fixed at once, so we fix the cheapest things that we can, that will help the most people first.

We are not losing any income, but the villagers will look at us, as if we are making changes to help them at our expense. A happy worker is a more productive worker. So, go over their lists and see what changes that we can make, that will benefit the most people in the shortest time. You can present the changes at our next meeting, as if you are helping pay for these changes. Do any of you have any other questions?

Earl of Kent: Changes that they will pay for themselves and increase our profits. You are indeed a wise Queen. The noblemen left the castle, sure that they could increase their wealth, under this new ruler.

James: I don't understand why the people have to pay for all these changes and the noblemen don't have to pay.

Kieris: Really! In order to raise an extra acre, they have to hire the villagers to clear the land, pay the store keepers for the extra seed to plant it and then have to give the villagers 10% of that acre too.

James: I should have known that you had a way for the people to come out ahead on the deal. The noblemen already pay the crown $400 each in taxes each year. The extra $40 from the noblemen will mean an extra $200, to help the people with each year. Plus, they will have to hire more storage buildings to be built, to hold their grain and buy more lumber, to build them with. The country will grow.

James put his arms around her: My beautiful, smart, and wise Queen, it is no wonder that the whole country loves you. He gives her a kiss and then just stands there holding her.

Bowen: Am I interrupting anything? James lets Kieris go and she laughs.

Kieris: No! Did you want something?

Bowen: To let you know that the villagers did not leave. They waited until the noblemen left and wanted to talk to you.

Kieris: Ok! Show them back in here and seat them at the table while I go freshen up. I will be right back. Bowen and Archer brought the villagers back into the room and seated them at the table this time. Kieris returned and sat down with them.

Kieris: Ok, who wants to go first? I will answer your questions the best I can.

Earl: We thought that we would be your advisors, but we saw that the noblemen would still be advising you. How does that help us?

Kieris: You are advising me as to what each village needs the worst, so I can work on those problems. We still need the noblemen to help pay for these changes. They think that they are using me, but that is not the case. Be patient, you will see changes and these changes will help the people. These changes will not come fast, it will take time, but they will come, and life will improve for all the villagers. I will continue to need your help, but we must let the noblemen think that they are winning.

Ray: What changes can we hope to see coming.

Kieris: First you should see an increase in the amount of work; you are hired to do for the noblemen. At the end of the year when taxes are paid, you will start to see improvements in the villages themselves being made. I don't know right now what the first improvements to the villages will be. We can't make improvements until we have the tax monies to do them. This country will start to grow, the villages and the people's living conditions with it. Be patient! Trust me! The villagers agreed to wait and see what happened.

They all returned to their villages to report that they had delivered the list and would know more in a week, when they returned for the next meeting. Kieris was worn out from the day and went to get some rest. Tomorrow she would sentence all the prisoners that the people had found guilty.

In the week that followed the last meeting, the villagers did start to get more work from the noblemen. They planted more crops, built more barns to keep the grain in and even built fences to keep the cattle out of the crops. The noblemen were pleased with the way their lands were starting to look but displeased that it was costing them so much to make these improvements.

15: The Lesson

After the advisor meeting, when the noblemen and villagers had gone. Bowen, Archer and James went hunting for tunnels. One of the maids that had taken a liking to Archer saw them walking around pecking on walls. Peggy: Hi, Archer. What are you doing?

Archer: Hi, Peggy. Don't say anything but we are trying to figure out how those men got in that killed the guards, because no one remembers seeing them enter the castle that day. We have heard of tunnels being in other castles and wondered if this one had any. We have to make sure the Queen and all of her servants are safe. Archer smiled at her and then she smiled back.

Peggy: Since you are over the Queen's security and do need to know, I will show you the one I know of. It is in the King's old chambers, it leads to the throne room and there's also another passage way out of the castle walls and into the woods. She took them and showed them where it was and where it came out.

Archer: Thank you. This is a big help.

Bowen: Other than us, have you ever told anyone of this tunnel?

Peggy: No, the few that know about the tunnels are sworn to secrecy. I only told you so you could keep the Queen safe. There are other tunnels, but I don't know where they are. The knowledge of each tunnel is passed down from one special servant to another when a new one takes their place. And of course they are known by the King and Queen who tell their children when they are ready to know of them.

James: Does anyone else know of this tunnel, that you know of.

Peggy: The King knows of it and another maid that the King used to bed all the time knows of it too.

Bowen: What is the other maid's name?

Peggy: Her name is Donna. She is a very hateful person and loyal to the King. I think she may even have a thing for one of the Earls. Most of the maids and cooks don't like or trust her, because she is mean and acts like she owns the place. She was upset when she found out that the King was going to marry Kieris instead of her. Archer caught her hand: Thank you again for your help. Don't tell anyone else about this tunnel or that there are any tunnels at all in this castle. If anyone else asks about tunnels or passage ways, please let me know. He smiled at her again.

Bowen: Tell Donna I want to talk to her in the library but don't say what it is about. Peggy nodded her head and left.

Archer: Kieris was too young when the Queen died so I don't think she told her about the tunnels.

Bowen: And the King was trying to keep her a prisoner inside the castle walls, so he would not have told her. James didn't say anything. He had an idea, but he would have to check on that later. Right now they had to get to the Library and talk to Donna. When they walked into the Library, Donna was already there waiting.

Donna looked at Bowen: I thought that only you wanted to talk to me. She smiled at him in a flirting way.

Bowen: No, we all needed to talk to you about something important. Donna acted disappointed: What do you need?
Archer: We were wondering if there were any tunnels in this castle like we have heard of in other castles. Do you know of any?

Donna got this evil grin on her face and walked over closer to Bowen. She tried to look all sweet and innocent, but it wasn't working. Donna: The crazy King seemed to like me, but never said anything about any tunnels. As far as I know, there are no tunnels in this castle. Bowen and Archer looked at James. James understood what they were thinking and then he mumbled something under his breath.

Bowen and Archer took a big step back from Donna and were making disgusted looking faces at her. Donna had been a pretty girl on the outside, no beauty but she was pretty and wasn't used to men looking at her like this. Donna: What is wrong?

James: We know you are lying to us about the tunnels, so I changed your looks. All the ugliness inside that you were hiding behind your pretty face can be seen by everyone now. Look in the mirror if you don't believe me.

She walked over to the mirror and looked in it. What looked back at her was the ugliest most homely hag she had ever seen. She put her hands on her face and began to cry: No one will ever want me now. I will never be married and have nice things.

Archer: Now tell us the truth!

Donna: Okay, there is one tunnel I know of, but I don't remember where it is. All I remember is that it starts here in the library and goes to the kitchen. Two big warts appeared on her face. Bowen pointed to the mirror. Donna looked again and saw the warts. She began to cry again.

Bowen: Your tears will not work on us. Donna looked at each one of them; they truly didn't care if she was upset over being ugly.

Donna: Okay, I will tell you the truth. I don't know if there is a tunnel in here or the kitchen. She looked back in the mirror and the two new big warts were gone. Donna: The only tunnel I know about is the one in the King's chamber. She looked again, and a few small wrinkles disappeared.

Archer: Where does the tunnel go?

Donna: It goes to the throne room. She looked in the mirror and a couple little blotches disappeared then a big wart came back.

James: You have to tell us the whole truth not just part of it.

Donna: Okay, the whole truth. It also splits off and goes outside into the woods away from the castle. The big wart disappeared.

Bowen: Have you ever told anyone else about the tunnel?

She didn't answer. Two big warts came back. Donna: Okay. I told a couple of the noblemen, but I am not the only one who knows about the tunnel. I don't know if they told anyone about them or not.

Archer: Who else knows about that tunnel? List them all and include yourself.

Donna: The King, I, all of the noblemen know

now, two of the King's special guards but they were killed when they refused to become eunuchs and a maid named Peggy. Donna looked in the mirror and some of the gray was gone from her hair. She still had a very long way to go to even look average.

James: Did the noblemen send the men in through that tunnel; the ones that killed the guards?

Donna: I don't know for certain if they did but if I had to guess then I would say yes.

Bowen: Later on the same day, is that how the Bishop got in without being seen?

Donna: As far as I know, the Bishop doesn't know about the tunnel, but he is friends with the noblemen and as long as it isn't against his religion, he will pass information to them. They could have told him where it was, so he could find out if Kieris was alive or not. Donna looked and little more gray hair, a couple more wrinkles and another big wart was gone. She had told them everything she knew, and she still looked ugly.

Donna: There is no more information I can give you that would be of any help. Will you please change me back? Another dark blotch disappeared.

James: That is up to you. The spell I put on

you will last the rest of your life. If you ever want to be pretty on the outside again, then you will have to change what is inside your heart. You must be kind, helpful, honest, and trustworthy to everyone. If doing these things is just to use them or help someone else to harm them in any way, then it is still ugly. Even if you become pretty again and go to doing ugly things, everyone will still see because the ugly inside will show on the outside again. She nodded her head that she understood and left the room.

Bowen: We cannot charge the noblemen for just knowing that the tunnel exists. There is no proof that they sent those men.

Archer: You're right but we do have to do something about that tunnel. We can't have anyone else coming in that way.

James: I have an idea. Get the material to make three metal gates and meet me in the tunnel. Bowen and Archer got what they needed and then went to the tunnel. James had them put up a gate at the three entrances to the tunnel and then he used his magic so that no one could open any of the gates except Kieris, Bowen, Archer, and himself, that way no one could get in that way but if they needed to use them, they could. They were all three tired and decided to check on Kieris and then go to bed. They would let her know what happened tomorrow and see if she wanted to do anything else about Donna. It had been a long day; they would hunt for more tunnels later and fix them like they fixed this one.

Early the next morning, Kieris called her brothers and James to her room. James, Bowen, and Archer all entered the room together. Kieris had told the staff to fix breakfast for the four of them and bring it to her room. It was ready and waiting, when the boys entered the room. They all sat down and ate.

Archer: This is good, and we didn't even have to cook this time.

Kieris: Being Queen does have its privileges. We don't have to do dishes either. They laughed and continued to eat. While they ate, they told her about Donna, the tunnel and what they found out.

James: I didn't tell her that I couldn't change her back, I just told her that was the only way she could change her looks. Do you want me to change her back?

Kieris: No, you three handled yourselves well and it sounds like it is a lesson that she needed to learn. James, I want you to find Donna and tell her that as long as she has the case of the uglies, I can't trust her and that she can no longer work in the castle, but if she gets rid of it, she will be welcomed back. Then without her knowing, I want you to adjust your spell to last only ten years, if she hasn't matured enough and learned her lesson by then, she never will. For the spell to last her whole life would be too cruel. James: Okay, sorry I didn't think about that at the time, but you are right, we can't be cruel.

16: Queen's Duties

Kieris: You were right that we can't charge the noblemen without proof, but I agree that we will have to keep a closer eye on them. After things settle down so I can, I will show you the rest of the tunnels I know about, so you can fix them too. I didn't think about anyone else knowing about them.

Bowen: How many more are there?

Kieris: Several but today we have something else that is important that we must do.

Archer: What?

Kieris: I need the list of who was found guilty; I will sentence them today and also give out the pardons. She dressed and went out onto a platform in the arena to tell the people what she had decided for each prisoner. She had each prisoner brought before her for sentencing. Bowen read out the case number and the name of the prisoner that it belonged to.

Bowen: The first prisoner is the old King of this country. You the people have found him guilty of murder, slavery, and cruelty.

Kieris: As Queen, I find the verdict fair. Since the King is in no mental state to be punished as other men might be; I sentence him to be locked up in a hospital for the insane, for the rest of his life, with no chance of ever being released. What is the next case?

Bowen: The next case is that of Merlin the Wizard. He was found guilty by the people, but they wanted you to grant him mercy, because he did help them when he could and also helped their new Queen.

Kieris: Merlin, do you have anything to say for yourself before I pass sentence?

Merlin: No matter what your sentence, I pledge my loyalty to you as Queen and promise to help you with this country in any way that I can.

Kieris: Merlin as your Queen, I order you to never do anything, that will hurt anyone in this country again. I charge you to obey and help me with these people. I pardon your actions because they were the orders of a crazy man, that you were sworn to obey. I give you the right to refuse the orders of any ruler, now and in the future, that would have you hurt these people or this country. I release you. What is the next case?

Bowen: The next case is that of Robert, the leader of the guards for deserting his job as a palace guard. The people found him guilty, as they did all the guards that deserted to save their son's lives. But the people also beg you, to show them mercy because all these men deserted to help save part of their family; and the fact that they helped free this land from the cruel and crazy King.

Kieris: I grant to Robert and all the guards that deserted to save their sons; and who also helped free this country, a full pardon. Who is next?

James: Next are all the guards that served the King, carried out the cruelty and even killed some of the people. These people included women and children. They have all been found guilty and the people beg that no mercy be shown to them.

Kieris: As these guards have been found guilty by the people and they don't want them showed any mercy, I sentence them to life in prison and hard labor for as long as they live. There will be no chance of any of them ever being turned lose again.

Robert: We the guards, the people and some of the others which you pardoned, ask why you are not putting them to death for these crimes. And the crowd also yelled why? She held up her hand for silence, so she could answer them.

Kieris: You the people have suffered for years because of their cruelty. Death would be too quick, and I feel that it is only fair that they should suffer as you all have, so they know how it feels. They will be punished the rest of their lives, plus by ordering them hard labor, they will be helping build this country. They will be forced to work building roads to make life easier, for all of you who have suffered so much at their hands. They will be forced to build bridges, so you can cross rivers safely with your families, goods, and livestock. Even after they have done all these things they will also suffer daily knowing that they will never be free but have to spend the rest of their lives locked up. The sentencing was over, so she returned to the castle to rest.

Later that evening the noblemen came to the castle to complain. Kieris meet with them. Kieris: I only have a minute, what is wrong now?

Earl of Mobile: These improvements are costing too much.

Kieris: How have you lost money? Yes, you are paying out more money to get the work done but the villagers that you are paying are now spending more money in your stores. You pay them and then the money comes back to you. By the end of the year at tax time, you will have made a large profit. Your patience will pay off even bigger then. I don't see the problem.

Earl of Carnes: I have seen the income in my store double since we started this, and I never thought about adding that into the factor, of losing or gaining.

Earl of Kent: What are we going to tell the villagers tomorrow at the meeting? The changes they want would cost too much.

Kieris: We will point out that changes take time and that they are already seeing changes. They can now buy more of what they need than ever before and that any changes to the villages themselves, will have to wait until tax time. When taxes are paid, we will have the money to start working on them.

Earl of Carnes: Do you think that they will be satisfied with that?

Kieris: Yes, I do. The noblemen left satisfied with Kieris's answers for the moment.

James: Kieris you are becoming a very wise Queen.

Kieris: I am worried.

James: Why? Things seem to be working out.

Kieris: I am afraid that the noblemen's greed will get the best of them. They have not thought about raising the prices for the goods in their stores yet, but I know that it is coming. That would undermine all the good, which has been done so far.

James: So, at the next meeting put a price freeze on all goods sold in the land.

Kieris: That may be a temporary fix; but for this country to grow, I have to get the noblemen to understand that they have to spend money to make money. Then there are the villagers, I would also have to freeze wages, so they could not charge more for the work that they do. These freezes could be a good thing or backfire on everything we are trying to do.

Bowen and Archer: Is there anything that we can do to help?

Kieris: Just keep an eye on the noblemen and let me know what they are up too. Bowen and Archer left the palace. James, I need you to do something for me.

James: Sure, what do you need?

Kieris: Draft me a set of laws that are fair to everyone. Visit the villages in a way that they don't know who you are and find out what they are up to. Oh, how I hate being Queen!

James puts his arms around her waist and pulls her close. James: Don't worry my love, we will work it all out; and remember this job as Queen is only temporary. You can do it better, than anyone else right now. (He kissed her.) Try and get some rest. I will see you in the morning. He walks her back to her room and leaves her at the door. She enters and closes her door, locking it behind her. For extra safety that night, because Bowen and Archer would not be in the castle, she goes into the secret safe room and locks herself in for the night. The guards are posted outside her bedroom to protect her. Once locked inside, she lies down but doesn't get much rest that night. As she had feared, the noblemen had called a meeting at the Earl of Kent's house the next morning, to discuss how they could increase their profits. In the villages, they were also discussing, how to make the noblemen pay the workers more for their work.

17: Tunnels

Kieris had to take her mind off of all of this, so the next morning she sent word to Bowen, Archer and James to meet her in the throne room for breakfast. When they got there, she had already had a variety of breakfast foods brought in and set up. They sat down and ate while they talked. Kieris: The noblemen and the villagers will be back here in the morning for the next advisor meeting. I need to take my mind off of things for a little, while so I can deal with them. I thought we four would spend the day together, (she giggled) tunnel exploring.

Bowen: Sounds like a great idea. The sooner we find and take care of safe guarding them the better. I will feel better when the castle is secure.

Archer: Yes, the safety of everyone in the castle may depend on the tunnels being locked up. Kieris, so how many tunnels are there?

Kieris: I don't know where all of them are, but I know where the ones are that the King knew about, because I watched him for a long time. That is how I found the safe room here in the throne room. The King and I were the only ones who knew about that one until I showed you three. Now that I am Queen, there are a few servants that I can ask about the ones they know of, they should tell me now.

While they ate, she told them where the ones she knew about were at and how to open them. After breakfast, Bowen and Archer went to work putting up the gates. James stayed with Kieris, while she questioned each servant one at a time. The first one she talked to was the head cook whose name was Pansy. Kieris: I need your help. Now that I am Queen, there are some things I need to know, so I can make sure everyone in the castle is safe.

Pansy: Anything I can do I will my Queen. I remember how kind and helpful you were as a child. I don't want anything to ever happen to you. What do you need to know that I may be able to help you with?

Kieris: As I said, this is for all of our safety, not just mine. I know there are tunnels in this castle. I know where a few are, but I need to know where all of them are, so I can make sure no one can use them to get into the castle and harm any of us.

Pansy: Of course, Queen Kieris you should know where all of the tunnels are, but the two I know of are probably not a risk to safety. There is one that goes from the library to the kitchen. In the library you go to the second bookshelf on the right, the third shelf from the floor and pull the forth book from the left at the top, that will open that end of the tunnel. In the kitchen go to the cabinet that I keep baked goods in, like cookies and breads; pull the left drawer out half way, put your hand in on the right side, at the top is a lever that can be pulled with three fingers, that will open that end of the tunnel. The King was the only person besides me that knew about this tunnel, but he is the only one who used it. Kieris shook her head yes that she understood where and how to open it, but the cook was wrong about who knew because she already knew about that one, she was more interested in the other tunnel, hoping it wasn't one she already knew about.

Kieris: The other tunnel? Where does it start and end?

Pansy: The other tunnel goes from the kitchen to the food storage pantry. I am the only one who knows where it is and uses it. It has come in handy a few times, to allow me to get to what I need without having to go the long way and deal with the mean guards.

Kieris: That is fine. You can show me later where that one is, and we will keep the location of that one between you and me.

Pansy: Thank you, you are a wise Queen. I don't know about any other tunnels, but I would suggest asking the head upstairs maid, the head downstairs maid and the head of the guards, because only the heads of each department are the ones trusted with the secret of the tunnels.

Kieris: Thank you so much for your help. I will let you know when I am ready for you to show me the storage tunnel. You can return to your kitchen now. The cook left.

James: That makes sense and will save us time if we only need to talk to the heads of each and that way no one else will think to hunt for the tunnels themselves.

Kieris: I agree. The food storage room is just an extension of the kitchen to me and the only person it can help is the head cook, so I don't want that one bothered.

James: We already asked Peggy about the tunnels before we questioned Donna. Peggy is the head upstairs maid, so we can rule out talking to her.

Kieris: No, I still want to talk to her just in case.

James: Ok, I will go get her. James left and was back in a couple minutes with Peggy.

Peggy: Your highness, I was told you wanted to talk to me.

Kieris: Yes, I understand you have already told James and my brothers about the tunnel in the King's chamber, which is good, but I need to know if there are any other tunnels, so I can determine whether they are or are not any risk to all of our safety. Peggy shook her head that she understood and then paused looking from Kieris to James and back to Kieris. Kieris: It is ok; I have and will always trust James and my brothers with my life. You can tell them anything that you would tell me.

Peggy: Ok. When I saw them hunting for a tunnel and they told me why they were hunting, I did tell them about the one tunnel, because it was the only one I knew of that led outside. I figured it was ok, but I have been wondering if I was correct in doing so, now I am glad to know that it is ok. I do know of two more tunnels which only the Queen and I knew about but they don't go outside. The first one goes from the Queen's chambers to your chambers. She would use it a lot, especially if you were sick, to check on you to make sure you were safe and okay. The second went from the Queen's chambers to a special safe room in the north tower. She told me if there was danger for me to take you to that room and she would come get us when it was safe, or if you both were gone for me to check there to see if you both were safe and then she would tell me what she wanted me to do at that point. I will show you exactly where they are whenever you are ready because they are hard to find even with directions.

Kieris: That is fine; I will let you know when I am ready. Thank you for your loyalty to me and your help. You may return to your duties.

Peggy left.

James: That was wise of her to only tell us of just the tunnel that would be a threat. I am glad you decided to talk to her.

Kieris: I am glad too. The Queen meant a lot to me. I can't wait to see her special safe room. Let's go to the tunnels where Bowen and Archer are; I will let them know what we have found out so far; while you seal them with your magic and then we can all have lunch together.

James: Sounds good because I am getting hungry. They went to the tunnels. When they were done there, they went back to the throne room to eat lunch. Bowen and Archer had built up a good appetite, so they had a big lunch. Kieris and James hadn't done much physically so they each had a salad with small pieces of chicken in it. After lunch Bowen and Archer, decided to join Kieris and James; that way if there were any more tunnels that were a threat, they could excuse themselves and get started on them, since they had already taken care of the other major threats so far. Bowen and Archer spent some time with Kieris, while James went to get the head downstairs maid. When James came back with the maid, they all were giggling about something and Kieris was blushing, James made a mental note to find out what that was about later.

Maid: I am Ruth your downstairs maid. How

may I help you, your highness? Kieris explained again like she did with Pansy and Peggy.

Kieris: Do you know of any tunnels in the castle?

Maid: Yes madam, I know of two tunnels, but I don't know if they could be used as a threat or not. My mind doesn't think about things like that. The first one goes from the main dining hall to the south tower. The second one has three entrances, it goes from the study and splits, one goes to the ballroom and the other one goes to the east tower.

Kieris: Thank you for your help. I want you to take Bowen and Archer and show them how to get into these tunnels, so they can check them out for me and then they can show me later where they are. After you show them, then you can return to your duties.

Kieris sent James to go get Robert; she had appointed him the head of her knights with Bowen and Archer over them. She wasn't sure if he would know about any tunnels, but he might know who she needed to ask if he didn't know. James left word at the gate that Robert was to come to the throne room as soon as he returned. He was out with a few other knights on patrol and wasn't due back for an hour, so James went back to the throne room and took advantage of some time alone with Kieris.

James: I left word for him to come here when he returns.

Kieris: That is right, I forgot about him being on patrol today. It is so hard to keep track of everything and where everyone should be all the time. I thought this would relax me some, but there are so many tunnels and just like the maid, my mind doesn't automatically think of them as possible dangers.

James: It will be ok, sweetheart. You have your brothers and me to think about these things for you. You are not alone, so you don't have to try to do it all yourself.

Kieris: I know, and I am glad I have all three of you, but it gets overwhelming sometimes. I know I can depend on all of you, but I still haven't gotten used to all of this. I knew this wasn't going to be easy, but I didn't expect it to be this hard. I still have to deal with the noblemen and the villagers tomorrow. No one can do that for me and I am not looking forward to it.

James was about to ask her what she had decided to do about the noblemen and the villagers, when Robert walked in; he would find out later.

Robert bowed: Sorry for the interruption, my Queen. I was told you wanted to see me and it sounded urgent.

Kieris: It is okay, Robert. In a way it is urgent, I need to make sure this castle is secure and safe for everyone inside. I don't know if you know the answer to the question I have, but if not, you may be able to help me figure out the right person to ask.

Robert: Anything you need, just ask and I will do my best to help, I am always at your service.

Kieris: Do you know of any tunnels here at the castle or who among the guards or knights that might know of any?

Robert: You have asked the right person and I agree that these tunnels could be a risk to everyone's safety. The knowledge of the tunnels was passed on to me by my father, because he used to be the head guard to crazy King Louie's father when he was King. Like the crazy King, the old King was mean and cruel, he didn't trust very many people and he trusted his son even less. Some of these tunnels, there is only two or three people that may know about them, but none of them know about all the tunnels. I know of three tunnels. The first and the one that is the biggest danger to the castle is the one in the King's chamber, it goes to the throne room and then outside of the castle.

Kieris: I already know about that one and it has been taken care of, that is the reason I must know about all of the tunnels, so they can be taken care of also, if needed. What about the other two tunnels?

Robert: They could be dangerous I guess. Both of these two tunnels split, and they have three entrances also. The first of these two tunnels has an entrance in the library, one in the stables and one in the dungeon. The old King would have his enemies, that he thought was a threat to him; captured by what looked like bandits, blind folded so they didn't know where they were going or where they were. He liked being in the library to read a lot, so he used the tunnel to meet his bandits, that had used the stable entrance, so no one would see them bring their prisoner in and take them out the other entrance into the dungeon and lock them up.

Kieris: I don't understand why he would go through all that trouble to capture them like that. He was the King at the time; he didn't have to have a reason to have them arrested, like his crazy son did.

Robert: I asked my dad the same question. He said that the old King was a little crazy and paranoid, but he didn't fear the common people or his noblemen, it was always an outsider, a duke, earl or visiting royalty that he would have captured. He would wait to see how much of a fuss was raised over them missing, if there wasn't much of an up roar he would torture and murder them. If there was trouble over them missing, then the old King and his bandits, who were his special guards, would knock them out and sneak them back out through the same tunnel and make it appear to everyone including their captives that they had rescued them. Everyone thought he was a great King, but he had the noblemen indebted to him because of the lands that he gave them to cover up these evil deeds for him.

James: I see, so because he was more cleaver than his son, he was able to hide the craziness that runs through their blood. It is a good thing that the crazy King never had any children of his own, it is hard to tell how nutty they would have been. But at least the crazy King had enough sense to adopt our beloved Queen. James smiled at her which helped lighten the mood for her some. Robert laughed: You're right, a child from that blood line would have been even more crazy, since each generation seemed to be worse than the last. They all three laughed, which brought another smile to Kieris' face.

Kieris: You are right, Robert. That tunnel would be dangerous too. If someone knew of it, they could have used it to get on the palace grounds. That could be how the ones who tried to kill me got inside and the one who killed them got in and out before anyone would know what was happening. A prisoner could get loose and harm someone in the castle or make it easier for them to escape. We will have to take care of that one for sure. What about the other one?

Robert: The last one could be dangerous too. The entrances to it are the throne room, dungeon, and the top of the west tower. The old King would use this one to listen in on others talking in the throne room from behind one of the pictures that hangs on the wall there. In another place in that tunnel he would check on his prisoners and listen to find out what they were saying when they thought no one was around. He also listened in on the guards when they were there in the guard house. Then he would go to the secret room that he had in the west tower to work on his evil plans so no one would know what he was up to.

Kieris: He was paranoid; because of it you are certain that the crazy King doesn't know about them?

Robert: Yes, my father said that the old King made him swear to never tell the crazy one about them ever, even after the old one was gone. My dad had me to swear never to tell him either, so no, there is no way he could know about them. Something else about the towers; everyone believes the old King had the towers built taller than what you could actually go up into to fool his enemies into thinking that we could see farther than we could and if they did get inside that they would be wasting their time looking for an entrance to a tunnel in the tower itself. There is supposed to be a tunnel that leads to the top of each tower and is the only way in or out of the top. The entrances are hard to find even with directions, so I will have to show you where they are and how to get in.

Just then, Bowen and Archer walked in. Kieris: We have two more problem tunnels that have to be taken care of today. Robert can take you to them so the three of you can start on them, while James and I take care of the ones you just finished. Start with the one in the library and we will be there shortly. Robert, you can wait there for us, so we know how to get into that one. After we finish with these two tunnels, I want all five of us to have supper in the throne room together. I have something I need to discuss with all of you.

Bowen: What about?

Kieris: First things first, tunnels then supper. They went their own directions after Archer told Kieris, in private, where, and how to get into the tunnels that Ruth had showed them. Kieris thought that Archer was trying to be funny with his step by step directions, like you would have to do for a small child, but now she understood. If you didn't slow down and take your time and do all the steps in order, then you wouldn't be able to get in. Kieris understood more now why Ruth didn't want to give her directions; she couldn't have done so without sounding like she was talking down to Kieris. Ruth was a wiser woman than she thought she was, because the mood Kieris was in, she would have taken offense to Ruth talking like that.

James sealed the gates with magic in the first tunnel and then they went to the other one. When they got in the second tunnel that had the split and went to the east tower, an idea came to James, but he would wait until they were in the tower to ask Kieris about it. They entered the tower and looked out the windows. All of the towers were made exactly the same, with a large window centered on each wall and the doorway was next to one of the corners. The biggest difference so far was the furniture that was in each one. This one had a long work table, a cot, a small eating table with two chairs, a dresser and a bookcase that was almost empty. This would be perfect for what he wanted to talk to Kieris about.

James: I was thinking that it would be a good idea for me to go back to all of the towers and use my magic to seal all of the windows, so nothing could get in or see in them, but we could see or shoot out of them if we wanted too.

Kieris: That is a great idea, that way if we are in here at night, no one could see a light or our shadows to know that there is a way into them.

James: I was also thinking that by sealing the room, no one would know if I was doing magic in here either. This room would be perfect for me to fix up my workshop in. It already has all of the furniture I need and would put me safely away from everyone to experiment with my magic and potions.

Kieris: Of course, you can have this room as your own, just don't hide away in here too long at a time, we don't get to spend much time together as it is. James pulled her into his arms and gave her a kiss.

James: Thank you sweetheart. This could be our place to practice magic together and so I can hold you in my arms, without being interrupted and steal some more of your sweet kisses. They kissed again.

Kieris: You are coming up with all kinds of good ideas today, but unfortunately, they are waiting on us, so we have to go. James gave her a sad puppy dog look. She smiled back at him: We have to go for now. He smiled back at her because that sounded like a promise of some alone time.

When they got to the library, all three of them were waiting on Kieris and James. Archer: Did I not give good directions?

Bowen and Archer looked at each other and smiled. Bowen: Yeah, I thought we were going to have to send out a search party for you two. What have you two been up to? Kieris blushed a little, but it was bothering James. It was one thing to pick on their sister in private, but not so good for them to pick on the Queen in front of one of her subjects.

James: I know you like to pick on your sister, but now is not the time. Using his eyes where Robert could not see, he motioned toward him. They got the hint and stopped, but it was really hard with Kieris blushing like that.

As they walked through the tunnel, Robert was explaining how to open each entrance to both tunnels, while James quietly sealed each gate. When they got to the dungeon, they left that tunnel and entered the other one. It didn't take Bowen, Archer and Robert long to put up the gates as they went, with James sealing each one behind them when they were done. When they got to the throne room, they checked to see if it was clear, stepped out to get a drink of water and the rest of the material for the last two gates. Bowen had put it there earlier, after Robert had told them where the entrances were; and Archer had taken the other supplies for both gates to the dungeon, just inside the tunnel entrance.

Kieris laughed as the guys headed for the tunnel. They stopped and looked at her. Kieris: You have already told me everything I need to know and don't need me to finish, besides I don't think I can climb another set of stairs right now. I would just slow you down. Kieris blushed again but her brothers and James knew she was taking the blame for her and James taking so long earlier. Kieris: I will order our supper and then lock the door from the inside, so you can come back through the tunnel. It will be faster, and I am sure all of us are hungry by now.

Robert: Thank you, your highness. I am starved because we didn't get to stop for lunch.

Kieris: Very well, I will order a big supper and you can eat your fill. Is there anything special that any of you want?

Bowen: Meat, vegetables, bread, and desert sounds good to me, doesn't really matter what it is as long as there is plenty of it. Archer, James, and Robert agreed with Bowen and then they went back to work.

18: Putting Her Foot Down

Kieris sent word to Pansy in the kitchen that she needed four hearty meals and one regular meal sent to the throne room for supper. She told the maid that she wanted a bowl of water, soap and hand towel brought back also. After the maid brought back the items for them to wash their hands, she locked the door. She went into the safe room and freshened up. When she was done, there was a knock on the door. It was their food; she helped them, set the table and arrange the food, thanked them and sent them back to their duties. She had just locked the door and sat down when the guys came through the secret door coming out of the tunnel.

Archer: Yes! I am starving. Kieris put up a hand and they stopped in their tracks. She pointed to the water bowl and smiled.

Bowen: Yes, mommy. We will wash our hands before we sit down to eat. They all laughed. Robert was starting to get used to them picking on each other. It was a sibling thing, nothing more. James had even let up about them picking on her in front of Robert. She was glad to see that they had bonded, because she trusted Robert and liked his whole family. Besides, Robert had already seen them pick on each other back at their camp in the woods and having kids of his own, he really didn't think much about it to start with. Robert had already thought that Kieris and James liked each other but wasn't sure. When quiet James stood up to her brothers to defend her and she blushed; he knew for sure but wasn't going to say anything.

After the guys had wolfed down about half of their meal, they started talking about the three tunnels that Robert knew about. They liked and trusted him, but the fewer people that knew about them the safer it was. When the meal was over Kieris cleared her throat to get their attention.

Kieris: Now, for the reason I wanted to talk to all of you. Tomorrow is the second meeting of the advisors and I am not happy with either group. I need to let them know exactly what I expect from them and that I will not be manipulated into playing favorites. I don't know how they will react to me being blunt with them, but it's time for me to stop holding their hands because they want to act like selfish children.

Robert: What do you need us to do? We are all here to help in any way that we can.
Archer: You know we are here for you. Do you want us to bang their heads together?

Bowen: Do you want us to shoot them in the butt with arrows?

James: Do you want me to turn them into

toads? They all laughed including Kieris. They could tell that the situation had her upset, because the more she talked about it, the louder she got. She smiled at them; she was glad they were here right now because she felt like she was about to lose it.

Kieris: No, none of that unless absolutely necessary. She didn't rule the idea completely out, because it kind of sounded like fun. She smiled again: I am not worried about the villagers, but I don't trust the nobles. I need all of you to stay close for the next week, just in case. I also want the knights to keep a close eye on the situation, just in case the two groups retaliate against each other.

Bowen: I will take two of the knights and we will watch the escape tunnel that the noblemen know about just in case they try to send someone through it.

Archer: I will do the same, so Bowen and I can take turns watching the tunnel.

James: One of us will be with you at all times, until we know that they are not going to try anything.

Kieris: Very good; but remember if they do, I don't want any killing unless there is no way out around it. They all agreed and left to prepare for tomorrow.

The next day, they were all back at the castle for the next round of meetings. They were all seated when Kieris entered the room. Everyone stood. Kieris: Please, sit down! (Her words were filled with anger!) I am disappointed in all of you. We should be working together to grow this country and make it profitable, for everyone. You will either, work with me or feel my wrath. They all looked shocked.

Queen: Noblemen, your greed will cost you in higher taxes, if you don't return the prices of your goods back to what they were, so the villagers can afford to buy what they need to live. The villagers chimed in, yes that is right.

Kieris: Villagers, you can't raise the prices of your labor to the noblemen either. You raise your prices, the noblemen raise theirs, and we are back where we started.

The land will not grow, and the villagers will once again, be starving.

Earl of Kent: If they don't want to pay our prices then they can buy their things somewhere else.

Earl of Mobile: If they want more wages then we will hire workers from outside this country.

Kieris: Silence! I am putting a freeze on the prices that the nobles can charge the villagers in their stores and also passing a law, that the noblemen cannot hire anyone from outside this country to work. (The villagers cheered.)

Kieris raised her hand for silence: Not so fast, I am also freezing the prices which the villagers can charge the noblemen, for the work that they do for them. Things in this country had just started changing and getting better for all of you. Then all of you had to get greedy. If these new laws are not obeyed, then I will take everything that belongs to the ones who break these laws. This land will grow and get better, with or without your working together. Now leave my sight. Bowen, Archer and James escorted everyone out of the palace.

Once everyone is out of sight and can no longer hear anything coming from that room, Kieris starts to break down and cry. James returns to find her still crying.

James: Are you all right? She is still crying.

Kieris: Why can't they just, learn to work together and help each other?

James: Don't cry! It will take time; they are all set in their own ways. Change takes time! She calms down and stops crying. She looks at James.

Kieris: You are right! Tomorrow I start looking for my replacement! James looks at her and just shakes his head. He knows, that her strong will and get things done attitude, is part of what he fell in love with.

James: Yes! The sun will come out tomorrow and it will be a better day. You will feel better tomorrow, but tonight you need your rest.

Kieris: Thanks James! (She smiled at him.) Make me a list of all the qualities a good leader should have. So I can find someone to take my place as ruler. Send the list to Merlin and tell him to start hunting for my replacement.

James: Ok. After she went to bed, he sat outside her room and made her a list.

1. Honest
2. Truthful
3. Stand up and fight, for what they believe in
4. Treat rich and poor alike
5. Defend the weak
6. Punish the guilty
7. Temper justice with mercy
8. Always be strong and fair in all dealings with others
9. Treat others the way that you would like them to treat you
10. Do not steal or cheat
11. Always pay your debts
12. Don't play favorites
13. Don't condemn others because they don't see things the way you do
14. Obey the laws of the land; if a law is unfair don't break it, legally change it

15. Don't let others tell you what to do make up
    your own mind

James smiled to himself, as he was making the
list. He left off the parts about a Queen being
beautiful and smart. He wondered if Merlin
would try to find a woman or man to fill the job
of ruler. Most women that he knew were selfish
and vane. Most men were greedy for money and
power. Kieris was truly one of a kind. Merlin
would have a hard time finding someone with all
her qualities. When he had finished, he sent her
message to Merlin along with the list. Merlin left
early the next day to carry out his queen's order.

James went and found Bowen and Archer, so
he could tell them about what had happened
and about Kieris crying. James: She is so
stressed that she is already talking about a
replacement. I am afraid that she is going to
have a breakdown, if things don't calm down
and start going right between the noblemen
and the villagers soon.

Archer: She needs time away from here.
Bowen, you and James cover for me and make
everyone think that Kieris is worn down and
needs rest. Don't let anyone into her room. I
am going to take her out through one of the
tunnels for some rest and to forget about this
place for a while. She needs to get away and
forget about being the Queen if just for a little
while.

19: Fishing Trip

Early the next morning James took Kieris her breakfast. After she had eaten he told her that Archer needed to talk to her alone and would meet her in the stables. She could use the secret passage to get there without anyone seeing her. It was important, and she needed to dress in common clothes just in case someone noticed her.

Kieris: What is wrong now! Why do I have to sneak away to meet him?

James: I don't know what or why he needs you to come to the stables, I just know that he made it sound really important that you do.

Kieris: I don't understand, but if you think that it is that important, I will go. She dressed in the old riding clothes that James had brought her.

When they entered the tunnel, James took her toward the one that led outside the castle walls.

Kieris: This is not the way to the stables. James just what is going on?

James: Archer said to bring you to the end of this tunnel and that is where he would be waiting on you. Kieris looked at James with a puzzled look on her face. She wondered if he was all right. She had been practicing some of the spells in Merlin's book too and cast a truth spell on James. James, are you all right?

James: Yes, there isn't anything wrong with me.

Kieris: Why are we going to the outside of the castle?

James: To meet Archer. He is waiting there for you.

As they neared the end of the tunnel, she could hear horses and Archer's voice trying to quiet them down. When they came out of the tunnel Archer smiled at her. Archer: I thought you needed a break. I thought you might like to go riding with me.

Kieris: She took a long deep breath and let it out slowly as if relieved. I would love to go riding and get away from here for a while. She turned toward James and thanked him. She gave him a hug and kiss. James: I will see you later. James smiles and goes back into the tunnel and is soon out of sight.

Archer mounts his horse: Are you ready? Kieris mounts her horse, putting her hood over her head, to hide who she is and nods her head yes. They rode toward the forest. After about an hour, they were deep enough that they were no longer seeing other people, so Kieris took off her cloak so her hair was blowing in the cool breeze and she could feel the sun on her face.

Kieris: Archer, where are we going?

Archer: I thought we would go fishing. We have not had fish to eat in a long time.

Kieris: Fishing! How are we going to do that, all we have are our swords and bows?

Archer laughed: I will show you how to fish with what you have. There is a shallow hole of water in the river that is right for fishing. No one ever goes there, so no one will bother us.

Kieris: Ok, if you say so. They rode for another half an hour and then stopped. The river was calm there, clear and you could see the fish swimming in the water. Kieris stood looking at the fish swimming. Trees shaded the water and it was cooler there. It was a really hot day but there in the shade it was just perfect, not to hot or too cold. Archer had brought ropes to tie the horses out, so they could eat after he had unloaded them. Kieris found a rock to sit on near the water and waited.

Archer: Are you ready for your fishing lesson?

Kieris: Yes! Now, how do we fish with bows or swords? Archer took one of his arrows and tied a string to it. Then he loaded it into his bow and shot one of the fish swimming near the bank.

He then used the other end of the string that he had tied to his boot to pull his arrow and fish back into shore.

Archer: See it is easy. We should have enough fish in no time to feed the whole castle at least one time. Then he laughed. Kieris laughed too.

Kieris: That is a clever way to fish. Do you have any more of that string? I want to try it. She got her bow and arrows as Archer got her some string. She started fishing too. Kieris: It is so peaceful here and relaxing. Thanks for bringing me. I really needed to get away for a while. The job of being Queen was driving me crazy. I really needed this! They both were not having any trouble catching the fish by shooting them. Kieris: I wish I had known that we were going to be gone this long. I am getting hungry and we didn't bring any food with us.

Archer: Oh, you of little faith. We have all these fish that we have caught we will just eat one or two of them. Kieris looked at him with a puzzled look on her face.

Kieris: How will we cook them? I am not eating raw fish! Archer smiled at her: I will do the cooking this time and the next time we go fishing, it will be your turn to cook.

Kieris: Ok. I have to see this; you are going to cook without any skillet to cook in. Archer just laughed and then started fixing them something to eat. He gathered dried branches that he could find on the ground to build a fire to cook the fish. Once he had fixed a place surrounded by rocks to keep the fire from getting out he put his wood inside the circle and lit the fire. He then used his sword to scrape the scales and cut off its tail up far enough for him to get to its insides. He then used his hands to pull out its guts making sure not to leave anything inside it. He then got two branches that were small enough to put up inside the fish and long enough, so he could hold the fish over the fire without getting burned. He then put one of the fish on the end of each pole.

Archer: Do you want me to cook yours too or would you rather try cooking it yourself? He smiled at her as she reached for one of the poles.

Kieris: Archer, you are amazing! I would never have believed that we could have caught fish this way or been able to cook them. They held their fish over the fire and cooked them.

Archer: The trick is all in learning how to survive with nothing. You have to learn how to use whatever is available, so you learn to think outside of the normal way of doing things. Where there is a will to survive or do something, there is always a way that you can find to do it.

Kieris: I will remember that! Their fish were fully cooked and ready to eat. They ate quietly, and he could see her smile as she ate.

Archer: How is your fish?

Kieris: It is the best fish that I have ever eaten.

Archer: There is one thing that you should remember, only use hickory or walnut poles to cook your fish on. Those two woods help give it a better flavor. Don't worry about it, if you can't find that kind wherever you are cooking because you can use almost any other hardwood limb to cook with, it just won't taste as good. But you definitely don't want to use an evergreen limb to cook with or you won't be able to eat what you cook at all. He laughed.

Archer had put all the fish that they caught on a string and placed them back into the cold water to keep them fresh until they got ready to return to the castle. It was getting late and was time to return. While Archer, got the horses ready so they could leave. Kieris used the leather hood on her cape to get water from the river and put out their cooking fire. Archer got their fish, and then they both mounted their horses and started back toward the castle. They did not go back into the castle through the tunnel that they had left through. They went straight to the stables where Robert and James were waiting on them. Robert took all the fish that they had caught. He would take them to the kitchen for Pansy to prepare tomorrow for them. He would let them think that he had gotten them for they didn't want anyone to know that the Queen had left the palace.

James escorted her back into the palace while Archer took care of the horses and then he would join them later. Kieris: I need a bath. I smell like fish. They both laughed.

James: So, am I to understand that you had a good time and are feeling better now?

Kieris: Yes, I had fun and I do feel better now. I guess we can wait a little while longer before we start looking for my replacement. I do want to see this country on its feet before I leave. He sneaked her back into her rooms where he had already had her maid prepare a hot bath that was waiting on her.

She went into her bathing room, took off all her clothes that smelled like fish. She put on a bath robe just long enough to give James her dirty clothes. She then locked the door and got into her nice hot tub of water. While she took her bath, James took the clothes and put them in with the other dirty clothes of his for the maids to wash. Then he returned to her room and waited for her to finish her bath, just to make sure that no one bothered her.

James had put a magical spell on the old

Queen's secret passages from her room into Kieris room so that only Kieris, Bowen, Archer or he could go through that passage. He also went and then removed the memory of that passage from the mind of Peggy the maid making it a secret again. He then told Bowen and Archer what he had done. James: That will give us another way to get into Kieris's room if she needs help that no one will know about. He would tell Kieris later what he had done.

It would be two weeks before she would have to face the noblemen and villagers again. The knights were keeping tabs on all of them to make sure that they were following the new laws that she had put in place. She was enjoying being the Queen. Giving orders to the staff and changing the way the palace looked inside. It was now brighter and more cheerful. At times she would order a large meal prepared and then when everything was ready, and it was time for her guests to arrive she would tell the staff that the meal was her treat to them. James, Bowen, Archer, and she would even sit down and eat with them.

Suddenly bad news arrived. The King had been very ill lately and had been put in the sick ward in the insane hospital. Late last night he had died. Kieris was very upset. He was a crazy man, a cruel man but he was still the only father that she had ever known. She started staying shut up in her room and avoiding everyone. The boys knew that this would never do, so it was time for some intervention on their part. The boys made plans for another trip away from the palace; but getting her to go was going to be a problem.

James would go to her door every day at meal time and take her some food. She refused to open the door for him, so he would leave it for her outside her door. When he returned later the food was still there. She had not touched it. He was worried if she didn't eat, she would get sick. Again, he went to her brothers for help. They had decided that enough was enough and she was going to see them one way or another. They entered the old Queen's chambers and through the secret passage entered her room.

The room was empty, and the bed had not been slept in. They knew that there was no way that she could have left the palace. The only passage that she could have used was the one into the old Queen's bedroom. They checked there, and that room was empty too. There had to be another passage that they did not know about. They all returned to the throne room to talk and see if they had forgotten something. They were each naming different passages and how they had found out about them. James: We found out about the passage into Kieris' room from the upstairs maid Peggy. I had forgotten there was another passage that she told us about, but I wasn't with her when Peggy showed her where it was.

They sent for Peggy, so they could talk to her about the passages. Peggy enters the throne room. Peggy: Good evening master wizard you wanted to talk to me?

James: Yes. I need you to show me the other passage way that is in the Old Queens bedroom. I wasn't with you when you showed the Queen.

Peggy: I am sorry sir, but the Queen ordered me to tell no one else where that passage is located.

Bowen: You don't understand my sister, which is, I mean the Queen is in trouble. She has used that passage to go to wherever that passage leads to. She has not eaten for days. We are all worried about her health and safety since the old King died.

Peggy: I understand but I cannot betray my Queen.

James: If you go check on her that would not be breaking your word. Take her some food and try to get her to eat something. Can you do that?

Peggy: As her maid it is my job to take care of her. That would not be breaking my word or her command. I will see what I can do to help her.

Archer: Please let us know what you find out. Let us know if she is ok.

Peggy: I will do my best and I will meet you all back here in an hour to let you know what I find out. She left the room making sure that they did not follow her. She fixed some food and took it into the throne after the boys had left to watch the outside of the Queen's chambers and Kieris' room hoping to follow Peggy to wherever Kieris was. Peggy entered into the secret passage from the throne room into the Queen's chamber and then into the passage that led up into the tower that was the old Queen's safety room. When she entered the room, she found Kieris sitting at the window looking out.

Peggy: Your majesty, I have brought you something to eat. James and your brothers are worried sick about you.

Kieris: I am ok. I just needed time to be alone and think. Thanks for the food I am hungry. Tell me what my brothers and James have been up to. She sat and ate the food that Peggy had brought her as she listened to what Peggy was telling her.

Peggy: They tried to get me to tell them about this passage and place but as you said it is just our secret. They are watching the out sides entrances to the old Queens room and yours hoping to follow me. But I tricked them. I used the Queen's private passage from the throne room into her chambers and then came here. I am sorry I had forgotten all about that passage, when I told you about the other ones. They are going to meet me back in the throne room in an hour, what do you want me to tell them?

Kieris: Tell them nothing. I will go back down to my room and clean up, then I will meet them there in your place.

Peggy: I am glad to hear that. I know that they will be happy to see you. They had kept your absence from everyone, even the staff. While you finish eating I will go to your room and run you a bath. When you come down I will show you the passage. Just leave the dishes I will get them later. Peggy left the room. Kieris finished eating and then joined her back in her own chamber.

Peggy: I will wait on you and go through the passage with you so they don't know how I got into your room.

Kieris smiled at her, took a quick bath for they didn't have much time if they wanted to beat the boys back into the throne room. As Peggy showed her the passage and led the way, Kieris noticed places where other tunnels might come into that passage. She would have to show the boys this tunnel, so they could check it out. When they got near the throne room they could hear voices. It was Bowen's voice talking to the Bishop. Bowen: How did you get into the palace?

Bishop: Don't change the subject. I want to see the Queen. No one has seen her for days. The noblemen and I have business that we need to talk to her about.

They soon heard the Bishop and Bowen's voices move farther away. Bowen still insistent that the Bishop tell him how he got into the palace. The Bishop was not going to tell him anything. Bowen escorted him to the gate and watched him leave after telling him that Kieris would meet with him and the noblemen the next afternoon. As soon as they left, and it was safe to, they left the passage and entered the throne room.

Kieris: We have a traitor and I am afraid that it is the Bishop.

Peggy: I agree! Oh, I am sorry; it is not my place to say anything. Kieris smiled at her: That is not an opinion it is a fact, you would not say that a dog was a cat. You would say that it was a dog. I will wait here for the boys. As Peggy left the throne room she met the boys in the hallway.

Archer: Well, what did you find out?

Peggy: Our meeting is in the throne room where there are less ears to hear us.
Bowen: After you!

Peggy: I am a servant of the Queen. All of you must enter the throne room first. It was hard for them to do that because they were always raised that ladies went first and, servant or not, she was a woman.

Peggy: It is ok, I have to get something. She was talking about the dirty dishes but didn't tell them that. She turned and quickly went down the hallway away from them.

Bowen: She is strange but cute. The boys entered the throne room and were greeted by Kieris.

Kieris: Hi! Come on in, we need to talk. The boys were stunned to see her but glad that she was all right. The Bishop has a secret tunnel that he can use to come into the palace. I think that he is a traitor.

James: We sort of thought that when he appeared today, and we knew that he could not have come in through the gate. How did you know? Kieris smiled and looked a little like she had a secret of her own.

Kieris: I know because the walls have ears even in here. Come with me! She opened the secret passage and the boys followed her inside. They lit the torches that were just inside and followed her down the passage way. She stopped where it looked like there might be some kind of door.

James: Where does this passage lead?

Kieris: This passage leads to my mom's, I mean to the old queen's chambers.

Archer: How did you find it?

Kieris: Peggy forgot about it when she was telling us about the other passages because no one has used it since the queen died.

Bowen: Kieris, Archer got to spend some time with you and I haven't. Would you go on a hunting trip with me while James and Archer find whatever passages are left and fix them so no one else can use them?

Kieris: After the meeting next week with the noblemen and villagers I would love to run away with you for a week of hunting.

Bowen: I will be ready and looking forward to our trip. Bowen had ordered the staff to bring a large supper to the throne room for them to eat that evening. Since Kieris hadn't eaten for days, he wanted to make sure she ate and had the staff to fix all her favorites. They had decided until Bowen and Kieris left on their trip that the safest place for her to stay at night was in the secret room behind the throne with them sleeping just outside the room. Kieris was doing a lot better and ate a large supper that night.

Before Kieris went into the secret room to sleep that night, James went into the room and cast a spell for the walls to show him any hidden passages into that room from anywhere else. The room was safe, the only way in or out of that room was through the door hidden behind the throne. They moved everything into the room to make her comfortable. Once she was safe inside and the door closed they had the staff to bring what they needed to be comfortable to sleep there. James also cast the same spell on the throne room but didn't find any new passages. He also used magic to seal the passages that they already knew about so no one could come in while they were asleep. After the staff left the throne room they locked the door from the inside and went to bed for the night. No one slept very well, all the boys had a very restless night. They were waking up, off and on, by every little sound that could be heard; except for Kieris, who was so tired that she slept soundly.

20: Laying Down the Law

The boys were up early the next morning. They had put their beds away and had breakfast ready when Kieris finally woke up and came out of her room. As they ate breakfast, they talked about what they were going to do today.

Kieris: I really don't want to be cooped up in the secret room all day and Bowen told the Bishop I would see him and the noblemen this afternoon.

Archer: That is easy, you will see them, and they can see you, but you don't have to deal with them. Bowen can deal with them, since he is the one that said they could see you. Archer laughed.

Kieris: What did you have in mind Archer?

Archer: They say that they want to discuss business with you and they are concerned because they haven't seen you in days. We will let them just inside the court yard without their guards. You can come out on the balcony and wave to them, so they can see you, then Bowen can turn them away.

Kieris smiled: I love it. I don't have to deal with them, besides I am their Queen not their servant. They have no right to demand that I see them if I chose not to. They could tell that she was getting upset so they changed the subject.

James: Ok, it is settled. Bowen and Archer will scout out the new tunnel between the throne room and the old queen's chamber while Kieris and I go look through my book of spells. We will meet back here for lunch and prepare for the Bishop and the merry men (noblemen) to arrive. They all laughed.

Bowen: They won't be merry when they don't get their way. I am already starting to think of just how to handle them too.

Archer bowed to Kieris: With your permission my Queen, let's get this hunt started. Kieris swung at him and missed. Kieris with a smile on her face: You may leave me now, to take care of your duty, my safety. Everyone laughed and headed off to take care of things.

James and Kieris went to the tower she had given him to use for his experiments and to practice magic. When they walked in Kieris noticed that the whole room was spotless from the ceiling to the floor. He had added a couple more shelves to hold jars with different ingredients for his experiments. He had made up the cot to sleep on, because he had decided to also make it his bedroom. At the foot of the cot was a wooden chest, Kieris assumed that is where he kept his clothes, since she didn't see any of them anywhere else in the room. Kieris began laughing.

James: What is so funny?

Kieris: This is not what I expected a master wizard's room to look like, especially a single one. Guys usually have to have someone to pick up after them and have stuff strung all over the place.

James smiled: I know but I like things organized so I can find what I want when I need it. I already told you about learning magic to help me with my cleaning for the wizard, Merlin.

Kieris: That's right; you did say you would make someone a good homemaker. They both laughed.

James loved hearing her laugh; it was like music to his ears. He went to the bookshelf and got his wizard book. They both sat down at the little table. James pulled his chair around closer to hers, so they could look at the book together. James: You look on the page closest to you, while I look at the other page. If either one of us spots something we can use to help find all of the tunnels, we can let the other one know.

Kieris: Sounds good, but we also need to keep an eye out for any spells that would help us with other stuff too. James nodded his head yes and then they started reading to themselves. They seemed to get done with their page at the same time, which was working perfectly until James started snickering trying not to laugh out loud.

Kieris: What did you find that is so funny?
James gave her a mischievous smile.

James: The spell isn't funny, but I thought of a way to change a couple of words, so we can use it for something else.

Kieris: So why is that funny?

James: Well, it could be to help us but that wasn't my first thought. I thought it would give us time to spend together and then I thought of some pranks we could pull on your brothers by using it.

Kieris: I am curious, but we only have ten minutes to get back downstairs for lunch, so you will have to tell me later.

James: Actually, they have ten minutes to get there, but we have an hour and ten minutes.

Kieris: I don't understand.

James: The spell is to stop water from flowing, to make it stand still, but we can change the words to stop time from moving. Can you imagine the pranks that we could pull on your brothers? That is what I was thinking when I laughed.

Kieris gave James a wicked smile: We could have fun with that one. They would never see it coming and there is nothing that they could do to stop it.

They decided to go on to lunch and then practice later, to make sure it worked, before they would use it to spend time together, because they didn't want to worry Bowen and Archer in case it didn't work. When they walked in the room, both Bowen and Archer noticed that they had funny looking grins on their faces. James and Kieris looked at each other and then shook their heads no. They would wait, even though it was tempting to try now.

Bowen: So, what have you two been up to?

Archer: Yeah, you both are acting weird.

James: We were laughing about some of the spells in the book.

Kieris: Yeah, some of them are useless. I don't understand what they would even be used for. But I guess if the right situation would come up that the spell would help with then it would make more sense, I guess. Let's eat, while I can. Just thinking about them coming here today, upsets my stomach.

They didn't say much during lunch because they wanted Kieris to eat. She had been having problems with her stomach and hadn't been able to eat much. After lunch, Kieris went into the safe room to take a nap until the Bishop and noblemen arrived. James stayed in the throne room and watched, while Bowen and Archer went to prepare for them to arrive at the gate. James was glad that Kieris was taking a nap; this waiting would have just aggravated her more. Bowen had Robert and three of the other knights posted just inside the gate, just in case the guards tried to force their way in. Archer spotted them first and gave the signal for everyone to get ready. James woke Kieris; she had a good nap and was in a better mood.

Bishop: Open the gate; we demand to see the Queen!

Bowen: The Queen has given us orders to let you and the noblemen into the courtyard, but your guards have to stay outside.

Earl of Cowan: What is wrong that our guards can't enter?

Archer: We have heard rumors of a traitor among us. She is only letting certain people inside the castle walls, so you may enter but not your guards. We are just not taking any chances that it could be one of them. They seemed to be okay with that explanation but weren't happy about it. They were surprised when the knights stopped them before they could enter the castle.

Bowen: As I said before, the Queen said you could enter the courtyard. Archer pointed to the throne room balcony. Kieris stood there waving at them, after she knew they had all seen her, she went back inside.

Archer: Now you may leave.

Bishop: What is the meaning of this? We demand to see the Queen now! We have urgent business to discuss with her!

Bowen: The Queen only allowed you to see her, so you wouldn't be concerned about her health. She said that if you had any manners and would have asked to see her, that she probably would have granted your request. She also said that she wasn't your servant to be told when and where that she would see or speak to someone. But since you tried to demand to see her like little children would, that you would have to be taught a lesson in patience and manners. None of you are allowed back here until it is time for the next advisor meeting. Bishop, she wants you back here then also. She has something important to discuss with you, but not until then.

They started to argue with Bowen, but thought better of it, when four more knights stepped out of the shadows and had them surrounded. You could tell they were extremely mad, but they didn't say another word. They slowly stomped their way back to the gate. They were not used to not getting their way, even the crazy King would see them if they demanded it. It wasn't a good idea if the King was in a foul mood, but he would still see them. They also figured if they brought their guards, that the castle would only have a few guards, Bowen, Archer and at most two knights, because the knights were always patrolling the villages. Once outside the gate and in the protection of their own guards, they all started yelling at Bowen, that the Queen would hear about how rude that he had been to them. After yelling for a little while and getting no response from anyone, they finally left.

James and Kieris had been watching just out of sight from the balcony. They could not make out exactly what was being said, but she couldn't wait for Bowen and Archer to come to the throne room and tell her. James and Kieris both busted out laughing when they saw them going back toward the gate. They looked like big children throwing a temper tantrum, kicking the dirt, stomping their feet, and acting like they didn't want to move. The only thing that was missing was the screaming and crying. Once outside the gate, then they heard screaming and whining but still couldn't tell what was being said. They went to laughing even harder then. By the time Bowen and Archer came in the room, James and Kieris had already been laughing so hard that they could hardly speak or be heard.

Bowen: So, I take it that you two saw and heard what happened. They finally calmed down enough to talk.

James: No, we couldn't make out what was said but we did see them having a temper tantrum on their way to the gate. They all started laughing. When they all stopped laughing again; Bowen and Archer told Kieris and James about what was said and by whom.

Kieris: Thank you Bowen. You told them exactly what I was thinking of but in a nicer way.

Bowen: Sis, I think this is a good time for us to go on our hunting trip. Are you up to that?

Kieris: Yes, the sooner the better.

James: Kieris, I will help you pack for the trip. From what I understand it is going to be really cold where you are going.

Archer: I will escort Kieris and Bowen up to the cabin at the middle of the mountain, where the snow starts, by horse back. I will bring the horses back and return in a week with them to bring you two back to the palace.

Kieris: So ,I will need snow shoes and heavy winter clothes.

Bowen: The cabin has already been stocked

with fire wood to cook with and keep us warm. A friend of mine will leave us some transportation the day before we arrive.

Kieris: What transportation?

Bowen: You will just have to wait and see. You need to get a good night's sleep because we will leave before dawn, so no one will see us.

21: Clues

They all returned to the throne room where Kieris told James she wanted to talk to him before she turned in for the night. They went into the secret room, closed the door, and talked in whispers so Bowen and Archer couldn't hear what they were saying.

Kieris: I am too excited to sleep. Do you think that we could try out that time spell of yours and have a little fun before we turn in for the night?

James: You really need to rest, but I guess we can go do one good prank before we go to bed. James used a spell to help Bowen and Archer fall asleep. After they were sure they were asleep; Kieris and James left the throne room through the new tunnel that would take them to the old Queen's chambers. As they went Kieris told James about how some places in the walls looked like they could be doorways. James used his magic to seal the walls just in case she was right. On their way back, he would do it again to make sure he didn't miss any of the walls, whether it looked like a doorway or not.

Once in the Old Queen's chambers, they cracked the door a little to see who was in the hall. The two guards that were posted outside Kieris' room were there, and Peggy was also sweeping the hallway floor. James chanted the spell and all three of them froze.

Kieris: Perfect I have an idea for this first prank of ours. Slide the spear out of one of the guard's hand, while I get the broom from Peggy.

James: Good idea. They put the spear in Peggy's hand and the broom in the guard's hand.

James: We can't leave the other guard out of our fun. James unfastened the other guard's pants and slid them down around his ankles. They heard the sound of someone coming and went back into the old Queen's chambers. James took off the spell, just as another maid entered the hall.

The other maid: Oh my! Peggy turned to see what she was looking at and then started to laugh as the guard was trying to pull his pants up. Peggy looked at the other guard who had her broom in his hand, then she looked at her own hand, when she saw the spear she dropped it.

Other maid: What are you three doing up here? I don't think the Queen would be too happy if she walked out of her room right now and saw this. The other maid left because she wasn't going to get in trouble if they did get caught.

Peggy: What is going on? How did you get my broom, why were your pants down and how did I end up with the spear?

Guard: I don't know but we better keep it between the three of us, because no one would believe we didn't make this up.

Other guard: What about the maid that just left?

Peggy: If she says anything, we will look at them and say she must be crazy. There is no way anyone would believe that we would do something like that.

Kieris and James kept their hands over their own mouths to keep from laughing. They went back in the tunnel, to go to the throne room. Kieris: Good prank but it didn't really stop time; it just froze the ones closest to us.

James: I will work on it while you are on your hunting trip. I will wait until you return for any more good pranks.

Kieris: Good, because I don't want to miss any of the fun. They made their way back through the passage with James resealing as they went. Kieris was now tired and didn't have any trouble going to sleep once she was back in the secret room.

James woke her up early the next morning

with her breakfast. She dressed, and James took her to the stable where Archer and Bowen were waiting with the horses. They rode out toward the mountains, along the way they saw wild turkeys, deer, and some rabbits.

Kieris: There was good hunting right here, why do we have to go so far?

Bowen: Because what we are going to be hunting for is not here. Besides if we are too close then someone might see us and then our trip would be over.

Kieris: Okay, your right, we do need to go farther away. I don't want my hunting trip cut short, but what are we hunting for that can't be found here?

Archer: That is a surprise and if we tell you then it wouldn't be a surprise. Bowen and Archer laughed.

Kieris: I guess I will just have to wait.

They rode in silence for a while then they stopped, killed three rabbits, and made lunch. Kieris: So how much farther do we have to go?

Bowen: Not much farther, we should be there in another hour.

Kieris: Ok. Can you give me a hint at what we will be hunting? Giving me a hint won't be telling me and won't ruin the surprise. Archer and Bowen looked at each other and nodded their heads yes.

Archer: Okay, I will give you one hint now and Bowen will give you one hint later. There will be no more hints after those two and there is no reason for you to ask for any more.

Kieris: Ok, what is my hint?

Archer: This animal has really long hair.

Kieris: That doesn't tell me anything.

Bowen: Yes, it does. It eliminates a lot of animals and almost tells you exactly what it is.

Kieris: You're right; it can't be a deer because they have short fur. I will have to think about this.

Bowen: That was an excellent clue, Archer. I will have to think about a great clue too, which almost says what it is without giving it away.

Archer: You will do fine, just watch your wording.

As they rode, Kieris started guessing. Kieris: Is it a bear? It has long fur and lives farther away.

Archer: No, it is not a bear, but that is a good

guess.

Kieris: Can I ask questions, like what color it is, and you answer me?

Bowen: No. Answering questions or even telling you if your guesses are correct, would be giving you more clues. Kieris stuck out her lower lip in a pouting look.

Kieris: You're no fun. Bowen and Archer laughed at her attempt to get her way. After a minute, Kieris couldn't help but laugh with them.

Kieris: Can't blame a girl for trying.

Archer: Nice try sis. They arrived at the foot of the mountain, at a small hunting cabin. They could hear dogs barking.

Kieris: What are the dogs for? Are they hunting dogs?

Bowen: Nice try sis. I will tell you they are part of our transportation to our hunt, but I will not answer yes or no if we will need them for our hunt.

Kieris: I thought I had you there.

Archer: I will go feed the dogs while you two go find something for dinner. We need to eat and go to bed early. I will head back first thing in the morning with the horses.

Bowen: Kieris and I will need to leave first thing in the morning too in order to get to our hunting grounds. Come on, sis. Let's see if we can find a deer, we can dry out the extra meat to take with us on our hunt. We won't have time to stop and cook along the way.

Kieris: Ok, whoever gets a deer first doesn't have to cook tonight.

Bowen: Deal, as long as we use regular bows and arrows. No unfair advantage. Kieris laughed: You're on.

A couple hours later, they came back with a nice size buck. Archer had a pot with water, potatoes and some wild onions with a few herbs boiling over the fire in the fireplace. All that was needed to make it a stew was the meat. Bowen was outside cutting up the meat, while Kieris went inside. The cabin had a small table with four chairs, a shelf with some cooking stuff and jars of herbs; Archer had taken their bedrolls and fixed up their beds.

Archer: So, what did you get and who got it?

Kieris smiled: I got a medium/large buck. Bowen is skinning and cutting the meat up now. What do you have in the pot?

Archer: Some vegetables and herbs, it is ready

for the meat to make it a stew.

Kieris: Sounds good. Thanks for making my bed. Since Bowen is outside and would never know, could you give me another little clue, I won't say anything.

Archer: No, but as long as you promise not to say anything, I will give you a clue about where you will be hunting.

Kieris: I promise!

Archer: All I am going to say is that you need to be extra careful because it is a dangerous place. No question, that is all you get, just think about it.

Kieris: Thank you.

Bowen walked in to hear the last thing that Kieris said. Bowen: What is going on here? Archer did you give her another clue about the animal we are going to hunt?

Archer: No, I didn't give her a clue about the animal. She thanked me for making her bed. You are welcome, Kieris. I made your bed too and started dinner for you. You are welcome, too. Archer acted like his feelings were hurt so Bowen wouldn't ask any more questions, because he wouldn't lie to his brother.

Bowen: I am sorry, Archer. Thank you for both

things. I finally came up with my clue and I was afraid our sister would trick you into giving her a clue without you realizing it. Then depending on it, I may have had to start all over to think of a new one.

Archer: Our sister is clever and smart, so I understand your fear, but I didn't give her any clue about the animal. All you have to do is add the deer to the pot to make stew. When Bowen was adding the meat, Archer winked at Kieris, she smiled and winked back.

Kieris: So, what is my clue?

Bowen smiled at her: After dinner. I need to make sure my wording is good first. I wouldn't want you to figure it out too quickly. Kieris nodded her head yes. She needed to think about Archer's clues, so maybe Bowen's clue would make more sense and make it easier for her to figure this out. Kieris opened up her bag that Archer had also brought in; she took out a loaf of bread that James had packed for her. Kieris was missing James already. They were starting to get even closer. She couldn't wait until this Queen business was done so she could find out if she and James had a future together.

Kieris: Here is some bread to go with the stew.

Archer: Thanks for bringing the bread. I like stew better with bread.

Kieris laughed: You can thank James when you get back to the castle.
Archer: I will do that.

While they ate their dinner, Bowen and Archer took turns drying the extra meat. After dinner, Kieris took care of the meat that was left to dry, while Bowen went outside to get things in order for his and Kieris trip and Archer cleaned the dishes. Bonding with her brothers was great. She was starting to learn about what she had been missing all this time. They picked and carried on with each other, but they also protected each other with their own lives. She wondered how different her life would have been if she had them in her life sooner. There was no sense in dwelling on what could have been; it would not change anything now. She was just glad they were finally all together.

Bowen came back in as Kieris and Archer finished what they were doing. Kieris: Ok brother, what is my clue?

Bowen: Just a minute, I want to talk to Archer first. Bowen and Archer walked over near the door and whispered back and forth for a couple minutes then they came back over and sat down.

Bowen: I was just double checking my wording before I told you. Your clue is; this animal is slightly smaller than a deer but has some of the same traits as a deer but isn't any kind of a deer.

Kieris: Your clue is more like a riddle. Thank you. This gives me a lot to think about. This has been a long day and if we are leaving first thing in the morning then I will need some rest. Good night. Bowen and Archer: Good night, sis. They all went to bed and were soon fast asleep.

The next morning, Archer was the first one up and reheated the leftover stew from the night before as breakfast. He woke up Kieris and Bowen, so they would eat too. They finished off the rest of the stew and started gathering up their stuff to go. When they went outside, they noticed it had snowed during the night. Bowen: Good, the fresh snow will make our traveling easier and tracking the animal a little easier too.

Archer: Be careful and have a safe hunt. It took us almost a whole day to get here and it will take a whole day maybe longer to get back to the palace, especially if you get any animals, so I will be back with the horses in five days to get you both. They said their goodbyes then Archer left.

Kieris finally saw the sled and understood now why they needed the dogs. She loaded their stuff in the sled, while Bowen got the dogs and hooked them up. Bowen: Make sure you leave room for you to ride on the sled near the back next to the handles. I will ride on the skids and drive the team, unless you want to drive.

Kieris: I have never been on a dog sled; much less driven a team of dogs, so I will leave it up to you. How far will we be going today?

Bowen: We will be going about half way up the mountain. If everything goes well, it will take about half a day then we can scout a little before bed and start our hunt in the morning.

Kieris: Will we be sleeping outside? I don't remember seeing a tent or anything. Bowen laughed: No, I forgot to tell you that there is another hunting cabin there. We will be warm and safe. Since we have to be back here in five days, we will only have three full days to actually hunt. You ready to go?

Kieris: Yes, I can't wait to see this animal we will be hunting.

They made good time in the fresh snow. As they went, Kieris was surprised how fast the dogs could go pulling a load up hill. In some places they had to weave back and forth to go up because it was so steep. This is the first time she had ever seen snow like this. It was deep and even clung to the trees. It was pretty, but colder than what she was used to. She was so glad James had packed some extra warm clothes for her. Every time she thought about James, she would miss him even more. She had to get her mind off of him; Archer had warned her that this place that they were going to hunt was dangerous. So, she needed to focus so she didn't get hurt or cause Bowen to get hurt. She tried to think about the mystery animal, but she was having no luck. The only animals that she could think of that could live in this climate didn't fit her clues. They already said it wasn't a bear, a wolf was too small, and a big cat didn't have long fur.

They arrived at the second hunting cabin right before lunch. They unloaded their stuff and then took care of the dogs. Even though the dogs were used to this weather, there was a lean-to for the dogs to be protected from the wind and snow that had started falling again. There was also hay on the ground to help keep them warm. They took turns in the cabin to change into dry warmer clothes. After they were ready, they took a hike up a nearby steep slope to a narrow path on the edge of what appeared to be a rock face that slowly went up. The path was very slippery, they had to take their time, so they wouldn't fall. The path got a little wider as they made the turn around the edge of the rock. Bowen motioned for her to be quiet then pointed along the rock face and up a little bit. There was her mystery animal. It was a mountain goat. Now all the clues made sense. Long hair not fur, dangerous place and horns instead of antlers; she had never seen one but had heard stories about them. She knew that they got a spicy meat out of it; some rugs and clothes were made out of their hair. She didn't like the clothes because they felt too itchy to her. All of these things cost a lot, now she knew why. It was really dangerous, and the goats didn't have any problem jumping around and playing on these icy rocks.

They started back down the path; it seemed to be worse going down than it did going up. She understood now and was glad that the bottoms of their boots only under the toes had small spikes sticking out of them. The spikes helped with the icy spots but slid easily on the rocks, so you would use the rest of the boot. Hunting these goats wasn't going to be easy at all. They finally made it back down to the cabin and warmed up.

Kieris: How are we supposed to get anywhere near them to even get a shot at them? They are quick and don't move in any predictable pattern. The steep rocks and ice doesn't seem to be a problem for them. They are very quick on that terrain. It was hard enough for us to get that far up and trickier getting back down. If we do get one and it doesn't fall all the way down, how are we supposed to get to it, get it down and still not fall ourselves?

Bowen: There are a few other things here in the cabin that will help us safely climb up and down the rocks. I will show you them in the morning and explain how they work. We are going for an older nanny goat without kids or an older Billy goat. You can tell their age by two things; they still move easily over the rocks but not as quickly and unlike deer that lose their antlers every year and then regrow them. Goat's horns just continue to grow unless they get broken off in a fight. They will still grow but they will be uneven, but you will notice how thick they are at the base of the horn. As they grow, they not only get longer but thicker to help keep them from breaking off so easily. I have never had one not fall all of the way down, but if it happens then we will figure it out.

Kieris: Ok, sounds like you have done this a few times. Let's eat and you can tell me more in the morning. I am too tired to understand much right now. They ate and turned in for the night.

22: Hunting Trip

Early the next morning, Bowen showed Kieris the ropes and pick axes that they would use to safely climb the rocks. He also explained how to use these tools. Bowen: There is a wide path above the narrow one that the goats travel every day close to where we were yesterday. There is a small rock formation that we use as a blind, so the goats can't spot us. We have time for breakfast and then we will have to get started, so we can get there and get set up before they come through.

Kieris: Sounds good. Let's eat. They ate breakfast and gathered everything that they needed and headed up the rocks.

Kieris was slow to start with until she got the hang of using the axes, but after a while she felt more confident with her climbing. They got to the blind about an hour later. They settled in and while they waited Bowen explained to Kieris a few other things about hunting goats. Bowen: We have about an hour before the goats get here. They will cross in front of us about here and go around the rocks there. We will wait until they are almost to us to make our first shot. They will continue on their path even if they are spooked for a short while and then stop to try to figure out where the danger is, which will put them closer to us for a second shot. After the second shot they will disappear before you can blink an eye, so make your shots count.

Kieris: Ok; anything else I need to know?

Bowen: Yes, because of their long hair, it is hard to tell if their leg is out of the way or just how big their body is for a side shot, or for a front chest shot, so you aim at the base of the neck as centered as you can tell. You need to pick one quickly then watch him as he moves to figure out where to shoot. If it isn't a kill shot, it would be almost impossible to track and find it.

Kieris: That is good to know, I would hate to make an animal suffer for nothing. About how much longer before they start coming through?

Bowen: Any time now. Suddenly the goats started coming into sight. Bowen motioned for her to take aim. They both shot at the same time. Bowen got his but Kieris missed. The hair made it harder than she thought it would, she had shot too low, but she wouldn't make that mistake again.

The goats moved a short distance, but they bunched up together a little more, which made it harder to tell where one ended and another began. Bowen motioned again, this time they both got the goats that they were aiming at. The rest of the herd disappeared before she could say anything to Bowen. These goats were faster than she thought. Bowen stood up and walked out of the blind, Kieris followed.

Bowen: Field dress them like you would a deer. Also, they have more than one stomach, so don't be alarmed that the guts look funny.

Kieris laughed: Ok. I will help you when I get mine done.

Bowen was done with both of his before she could get done with her one. The hair kept getting in the way. Bowen started laughing and Kieris gave him a dirty look. Kieris in an aggravated voice: Are you going to help me or are you just going to stand there and laugh?

Bowen: Ok, let me show you. He knelt down and showed her how to keep the hair out of the way while he worked on it. He was done in no time. Bowen: Next time you get to do it all by yourself.

Kieris: Thank you. Nothing about this hunting trip has been as easy as it seems. I can't believe I missed that first goat, I thought his body was bigger than what it was and shot a little low.

Bowen: It's okay. My first-time hunting, I missed both shots, at least you got one your first time out.

Kieris: Thanks for that. How many more do we need?

Bowen: At least three more, we can get them tomorrow. Right now, we have to get these three down.

They took the goats near the edge as close to the cabin as they could and shoved them over. They started back down, this time it wasn't as scary. When they got to the bottom, Bowen untied the rope that he had used to tie him and Kieris together while they were climbing. They left the axes there and took the ropes with them. They tied the ropes to the goats, sliding them back to the cabin together which was easy to do on the snow and ice. Then they hung them up. Kieris went back after the axes, while Bowen started to skin the goats. He had two of them skinned by the time she got back.

Bowen: I saved one, so I can show you the easy way to do this and keep the hair out of the way.

Kieris: Thank you. He showed her how and then they hung them up inside a room to start to tan the hide, so they wouldn't lose any of the hair. They both cut the muscles off the bones, put them in a pile on a clean hide, so they could take them inside to cut up the meat and wrap for their trip back.

When they were done with that, Kieris cooked

dinner while Bowen moved the bones away from the cabin, so it wouldn't draw any bears, wolves, or big cats to the cabin. They ate dinner and went to bed. Early the next morning, they ate breakfast and headed out to hunt again. This time Kieris got both of hers and Bowen only got one. Kieris knew Bowen missed on purpose so she would not feel bad about missing one yesterday, besides they only needed six goats, there was no reason to waste any. This time, Kieris and Bowen worked together tanning the hides and cutting up the meat after dinner. Kieris never tanned hides before; she was learning so much from her brother. There was another snow storm moving in, so they got everything ready to leave in the morning.

The next day, they took their time going back to the first hunting cabin because the storm wasn't moving in as fast as they thought it would. On their way, Bowen told her stories about their parents and uncle. This was a hunting trip that she would never forget. Archer was waiting on them when they got back to the other cabin. He had come back early because of the storms; he was worried about them. He had brought a wagon back with him to carry the hides and meat back. Since they had the extra day, the three of them spent the time telling stories and just getting to know each other better. This had turned into a family outing; except James wasn't here. They all felt like he was part of their family too. They had a great day together; if it wasn't for missing James she would rather for them to stay right here. They got everything ready to leave in the morning, ate dinner and went to bed.

Leaving early the next morning and on their way back to the castle, all Kieris could think about was James. She couldn't believe just how much she missed him. She hoped that he had been practicing the time spell. She couldn't wait to pull a couple of pranks on her brothers. Kieris: Right before we get to the first village, that we have to go through to get back to the castle, I want to separate the meat. I want to pick out just enough for the castle. Then some of it can be given to the widows and the orphans in each village by the knights as they are making their patrol rounds.

Archer: That is a great idea!

Bowen: I had an idea for the hair, which is the reason I wanted so many goats. I thought that some of the clothes makers could blend the goat hair with the cotton that they already use making it warmer and make all of the orphans a coat for this winter.

Kieris: Perfect! I love the idea.

When the knights go to the orphanages to leave the meat, they can get the number of orphans and sizes the coats need to be. They made it back to the castle, just in time to get cleaned up and have dinner with James. She hurried to get ready; she couldn't wait to see him and tell him about her adventure hunting mountain goats. They all arrived at the throne room about the same time. It was good for them to be all together again. The cook sent them a variety of meats for them to eat, Kieris was glad she had a choice. She liked the spicy meat, but she had already had her fill of it before they got back. She didn't put any on her plate and neither did Bowen.

James: Remember exactly where you are and what you're doing. Kieris looked up, everyone was perfectly still.

Kieris: So, you have been practicing while I was gone. Are they just frozen or has time actually stopped?

James smiled at her: Come to the window and look. They went to the window. Everyone below was frozen too; even a bird just outside the window was frozen in midflight.

Kieris: How do you know if time has really stopped or if they are just frozen at a farther distance?

James: I froze time and wondered the same thing, so I went for a walk. I walked for two days and came back; everything was still exactly the same. When I unfroze time, I checked on the people to see how they were acting after being frozen for so long and everyone was all right.

Kieris turned and looked at her brothers and smiled. Kieris: This is perfect for our first prank. Switch the food on Archer's fork with something that isn't on his plate, something you think he won't like. I already know what I am putting on Bowen's fork. James smiled and helped her switch things. When they were done, they sat back down and picked up their forks. Kieris nodded her head to let James know she was ready and he unfroze time.

Bowen: I have eaten so much goat meat, that everything tastes like it now. Archer spit his mouthful out, James had put spinach on his fork and he didn't like any green vegetables except lettuce.

Archer: Yuck, how did I get a bite of this? I don't even have any on my plate.

James froze time again. James and Kieris, both busted out laughing. Kieris: This is great.

James: I have a better idea. Help me move Bowen and his chair where Archer is at and then we will move Archer where Bowen is at.

Kieris laughed again: I love it, let's do it. They moved them both and then sat back in their own chairs. Kieris: I am getting hungry, so let them wonder a little bit before we tell them.

James: Ok, I am getting hungry too. Are you ready?

Kieris: Yes. James unfroze time.

Archer: Wait a minute; this isn't where I was sitting or my plate.

Bowen: Mine isn't right either, and somehow, we have traded places. They looked back at each other with a confused look on their faces.

Bowen and Archer switched plates and ate their food in silence. Something wasn't right here but no one seemed to notice except Bowen and Archer. When they were all done eating, Kieris looked at Archer and smiled. Kieris: What is wrong Archer? You have this weird look on your face.

Archer: Yes, something is going on and I am trying to figure out what it is.

Bowen: Yes, wrong food, plate and even my chair is in the wrong place. I thought I was going crazy for a minute, until Archer's had all changed too.

Kieris: I was so busy eating that I thought you two changed chairs trying to play a prank on me. James and Kieris laughed.

Archer looked at James just as he figured it out. Archer: Bowen, these two have been pulling pranks on us.

Bowen: How? James looked at Kieris; because he didn't know how much she wanted them to know just yet, so he was leaving it up to her to tell them what she wanted them to know.

Archer and Bowen looked at Kieris too. Archer: Ok little sis, how did you do it?

Kieris: Sorry, I could not help myself. She laughed. James helped me by using a little magic; I hope that you are not mad. I needed a few good laughs before I face the noblemen and Bishop tomorrow. The boys both laughed, they were not mad. They all got ready and went to bed for the night.

She was still having problems with the noblemen and bishop trying to take her throne. There was unrest in the land as the threats to Kieris life continued. Kieris had decided to put an end to there being any traitors against the throne and the ruler of the country. She wanted whoever took over her job to be safe. When the noblemen, villagers and Bishop arrived the next morning they were all sent into the courtyard where Kieris could talk to all of them at the same time. Once they were all in the courtyard, Kieris went out on the balcony to talk to them.

Once she appeared all the noblemen and the bishop began yelling and demanding that she give them a private meeting with her. She went back inside without saying a word.

Bowen went out and told the crowd: Be quiet. The Queen has something to tell all of you and you better listen to her. When she comes back out I want there to be silence. As he was talking the knights had surrounded the crowd to ensure that they listened. As before the noblemen's guards had not been allowed inside the palace gates so they all got quiet. Kieris returned to the balcony and everyone was quiet.

Kieris: First I am not your slave. You have no right to demand that I meet with you or anything else. I am your Queen! Some of you have turned against my ruling this country and then again some of you have always been against me being your Queen. I will not be Queen much longer. There has been a search going on for a long time to find someone to replace me. You will not choose your new ruler, and neither will I. Merlin has been hunting and will soon find my replacement. The laws that are in place will stand and be obeyed but I am passing a new law today. I wanted you all to hear it, so you can't say that you didn't know.

Anyone found plotting against the throne, trying to kill the ruler or just being a traitor to this country will be brought to trial. And as in the first trials, the people will not know who they are voting not guilty or guilty, so they can't play favorites or be paid to vote them not guilty. Make no mistake; no one is above this new law. Bishop let's say that you are found guilty or a member of the priesthood. The punishment would be the same as for someone who came here from outside this country and tried to kill me. Bishop if you were found guilty you would be put to death. Breaking this law doesn't mean just trying to kill the ruler or over throw him. It also means just plotting to harm the ruler. That person will get the same punishment. Bishop, that law would also mean anyone sneaking others into the castle to do harm. Don't be surprised if there are not arrests made in the next few days for some of the crimes that have already been committed. This is just an example but it shows that the Bishop, Nobleman, outsiders, or common people are not above this law.

Kieris went back inside without another word leaving the crowd looking confused. Had the Queen just accused the Bishop of the crimes that she named? They all left the castle grounds confused and wondering. Once inside James put his arms around her: The scared look on the Bishop's and some of the noblemen's faces said it all. You made your point. They were scared enough that some of them may even leave this country, afraid that you already know exactly who they are and what they have done. Kieris had sent men, to find Merlin and let him know, that she would like to talk to him. James had become a first-class wizard and could now control all, of Merlin's old magical spells and had created a few new ones, of his own. Bowen and Archer were still the best bow and arrow makers in the land. Kieris, Bowen and Archer were still the best bow shooters in the world. Kieris had decided that it was time for a new leader, so she could be free of this job.

23: Merlin's Return

One year had passed since she had become queen; the noblemen and villagers were finally working together, and the country was growing. Word had come that Merlin had gotten her message and was on his way back to the palace to see her. He was bringing with him, an extra special gift for the Queen. It was a one of a kind sword called Excalibur, given to him by the sorceress of the Great Lake Superior, in the country of America. The gift was to help the Queen find a new ruler and her replacement. James woke Kieris early the next morning and informed her that Merlin would be arriving soon. She was excited! She dressed in the clothes of a peasant and waited in the ballroom with the noblemen's and villager's wives, and their servants. When Merlin entered the room, he walked past the others, straight to Kieris and knelt down on one knee, at her feet. Merlin: My Queen!

Kieris: Rise! How did you know?

Merlin smiled: You are the only one in the room who really doesn't want to be here. May we talk in private?

They left the others and went into the throne room where Kieris sat down on the throne, to listen to what Merlin had to say. Merlin: I have a gift for you! He handed her the sword. She took it and looked at it as Merlin told her about the sorceress and the sword. The sorceress had told him that only Kieris could use the sword and if she decided to give up her throne; she could take it to the Great Rocky Mountains, who was the father of time and push it into the great rock wall, asking Father Time to hold it for her. She could not, as Queen, give it up to just anyone. The only person who would be able to pull it back out was Kieris, or whoever the sword found worthy enough to take her place.

Kieris: How do I know that she can be trusted, and this is all true?

Merlin: Allow James to travel with me and test her.

Kieris: How long will it take to do this? She hands him back the sword.

Merlin: Traveling by magic, only a few minutes.

Kieris: Wait here! She leaves the throne room and goes to where James is and tells him what has happened.

Kieris: What do you think that I should do?

James: We need a code, in case something is not right. Here cast this spell on me, and then I will go with Merlin. Kieris had been learning magic too and was pretty good at casting spells herself. She read the spell casting it on James and then they returned to Merlin and the throne room.

Kieris: I have brought James to go with you, see that he returns safely. I will wait here for the two of you. Merlin cast a spell and they both disappeared. James found himself standing on the edge of a huge lake with Merlin.

Merlin: Lady! Lady! We have come to visit and so that you could tell my young friend, what you told me about the sword. The water shimmered; a beautiful woman rose out of the water and seemed to float on top of it, over near the land that they were standing on.

Lady: Merlin, I see you have brought my son, James to see me.

James: Your son?

Lady: Yes! Merlin took you away as a baby, to raise you in the ways of magic. Merlin did not tell you that I was your mother and that he is your father?

James: No, he did not!

Lady: James, hear what I have to tell you now. The time has come for you to know the truth. Kieris will make you a perfect bride and a good wife, but her job as Queen must end. The country you now live in is going to be in a great war and part of that war will be to find a new leader. She will no longer be able to rule this country. The sword will do just what Merlin said. Once she has placed it into the great rock wall, only the new ruler will be able to pull it out again. Merlin will help and guide this new ruler, so he can carry on the great work that Kieris has already started.

James: Then Merlin has only told her a half truth. He told her that she could pull it back out herself, if she wanted to.

Lady: I am afraid that she can do that, but she must never pull the sword back out of the hands of Father Time. When things start to go bad, she will think that she has too and that by pulling it back out herself she can help. If she pulls it back out herself, it will only mean her death.

James: I cannot lie to her! I love her and don't want to see her die. If she knows that she will not be able to pull the sword back out, she will not put it into the wall to start with.

Merlin: If she doesn't, then she will die.

Lady: James, if you think that it will help, then I will talk to her.
James: No! Mother, I will have to do this myself, even if it means that she will never forgive me. In a hurt and disappointed tone of voice, he told Merlin that he was ready to go

back. Once back in the throne room, Kieris could see the hurt and sadness in James' eyes.

Kieris: Well, what did you learn? James thought to himself, to choose his words carefully. The spell that he had gotten her to put on him, would not allow him to lie to her.

James: I found out that the best thing for the country and you is for you to put the sword into the great stone wall. Kieris knew that the spell that she had put on him, before he left, would not allow him to tell a lie to her, so what he said must be the truth. She still wondered what was troubling him.

Merlin: There is one more thing, which I have not told you yet. The day that you push the sword into the stone wall, you will be transported from this country.

Kieris: What?

Merlin: You will no longer be able to help this country or these people. So, for your safety, and the safety of the ones you love; Bowen, Archer, James, and you, will be magically transported to the country of America.

Don't worry I will be staying here to help the new ruler. Keep him on the right path and to keep him helping this country and all its people.

Kieris: James?

James: I will stand by you no matter what choice you make. To the death if needed!

Kieris: Merlin you will have my decision in the morning. Merlin handed her back the sword.

Merlin: Here, either way right now, the sword is yours. Yours to keep as is the job of Queen or yours to give to a new leader for this country. Merlin leaves the room.

Kieris tells Bowen and Archer, to meet her in her room, in one hour. Oh! James you come too! Kieris leaves the room and returns to her suite. She is seated on the sofa when the boys arrive in her room.

Kieris: James seal this room so no one but the four of us can hear whatever is said in here and make sure Merlin can't hear us either. James did what Kieris asked him to do. Once the room was sealed they began to talk.

Bowen: What is up, sis!

Archer: Yes! You seem really upset!

Kieris: Ok! James, the spell you had me put on you, before you went with Merlin was so that you could not lie to me, even if they tried to make you. So, what you said had to be the truth; but your eyes and manners told me that you were leaving out things, that you did not want to tell me. I want to know everything, that happened and everything that they told you.

James: Ok.! We went to see the lady of the lake. She really lives in the great lake. She told me that I was her son and that Merlin was my dear old dad. (You could hear the sarcasm in his voice.) They told me that your days as ruler were about over. That if you didn't put the sword in the great rock wall, in the hands of Father Time, that you would die. They also said that if you pulled it back out of the great rock wall after you put it in, you would die. They told me that there was a great war coming and that you could not help this country or these people anymore. The war would help decide who the new ruler would be. The only real choice that you have is whether to put the sword in the rock wall and live, or don't put it there and die.

Kieris: Some choice!

Bowen: Look on the bright side, either way your job as Queen will be over. Everyone looked at him like he was crazy, then all of a sudden Kieris started laughing. Now they were all laughing!
Kieris: Ok! We will go to the great rock wall tomorrow and end this job. I am tired of being Queen anyway and I am sure that I don't want to die.

The next morning, she addressed the people of the land. Kieris: My loyal followers, I am leaving on a long journey. While I am gone I am leaving Merlin in charge. He will guide you and find you a new ruler to help build this land while I am gone.

They all went back inside and re-dressed in the clothes that they had on when they first met, and left the castle by a secret passage, so no one would follow them. Merlin took them all to the great rock wall, also known as Father Time, and handed Kieris the sword that he had carried there for her.

Kieris: Rock Wall, I mean Father Time, as Queen I command you to hold this sword and let no one else be able to pull it from you, unless he is the right person to rule this land.

The great rock wall started to move, and a giant rock man sat up and spoke to them.

Father Time: As you are the Queen of this land right now, with an honest heart and have done so much for the people of this land, I will honor your request. He reached out with one of his big stone hands and Kieris laid the blade of the sword in his hand. He shut his hand, leaving only the handle of the sword sticking out. They all together, including Merlin, repeated the spell which she had said as she put the sword into Father Time's stone hand to help seal it there. Father Time laid back down and all signs of the giant disappeared. All that could be seen was the rock mountain and the handle of the sword. Then Merlin chanted a spell on Kieris, Bowen, Archer and James, and they all disappeared except for Merlin.

Merlin: Goodbye, my son. Goodbye, Master Wizard. Take care of Kieris and her brothers. Take care of your new wife to be and your two best friends. This journey has ended, but for you four a new journey has just begun. Merlin had sent them through space, to the Americas and landed them, beside the Great Lake Superior and near the Lady of the lake. It would now be her turn, to help their son.

24: New Ruler

A great war broke out in the country and Merlin told the people of the land that whoever was able to pull the sword from the stone, would be their new King. The people traveled to the great rock wall, from all over the country to try their luck and to try pulling the sword out, of the stone. Most of them came because they wanted to be King, rule and be rich. Others came just to try and get rich. As each man tried and failed to pull the sword out, they tried to come up with other ways, to remove it from the stone. Some had even tried, to chip the rock from around it, so they could get it out. But nothing that they tried worked. Between Father Time's hold on the sword and the magic that had sealed it there, the stone was solid and could not be broken.

While all these men were trying to get the sword, Merlin was hunting for someone pure of heart, that he could help become the new ruler, of this country. The war was over for now and the only conflict was over who would be the new ruler of this land. All the men were already set in their ways and were either power hungry or greedy. So, Merlin had turned to the young boys in the country, to try and find a new King.

Meanwhile, back in America, James, Bowen, and Archer had all three built themselves, homes near the lake. James and Kieris had gotten married, with the blessing and help from the Lady of the Lake. James and Kieris both now practiced magic and were happy. Bowen and Archer had traveled for a while, before they built their homes and had also married. The lady of the lake watched over and protected them all.

Each morning at sunrise, when the sun touched the handle of Excalibur, the sword would sing but no one could hear it, except Father Time, Merlin and the boy who would become the next King. The boy had heard the sword every morning, since he had turned twelve years old. After asking his parents, where the beautiful music was coming from and being told that they didn't hear anything, he kept the fact that he was hearing the singing of the sword to himself. He was afraid; they would think that he was crazy.

Merlin had searched for the boy for several years and had not found him. Arthur was not sixteen years old yet, but had traveled with his father and brothers, to the granite mountain which was Father Time, so his father and brothers could try their luck at pulling the sword from the stone. His father had told him, he was too young to try, so he would just get to watch. Jerry was only his adopted dad; they had taken him in as a baby, when they found him alone with his mother's dead body. He never knew that Jerry was not his real father and his brothers were only his because the family had adopted him.

They had been at the mountain, Father Time, for three days; but had to wait their turn to try for the sword. Whoever could pull the sword, from the stone would be made King. Jerry was hoping that if he could not pull the sword out himself, that at least one of his sons could. One night, while the rest of the camp slept, Arthur was restless, so he got up and went for a walk. When he got near the sword, he could hear it singing. It was the sound of the beautiful music that he had heard for so long and wondered where it came from.

No one was around, so he moved closer to the sword. The closer he got to the sword, the better he could hear the sword singing. He caught hold of the sword and it slipped out of the rock. He could now hear people moving around in the camp and it scared him. He pushed the sword back into the rock and left just before they started gathering, so the next man could try to pull it out.

It would soon be time for his dad and brothers to try and pull it out. He called his dad over to the side. Arthur: Dad, I can pull the sword from the stone.

Jerry: What makes you think that you can, when no one else has been able to? Your brothers will try in the morning and they are all stronger than you are.

Arthur: I know that I can, because I pulled it out last night, while everyone else was asleep.

Jerry: You what? Boy, are you lying to me?

Arthur: Father, I have never lied to you and I am not lying this time.

Jerry: Don't tell anyone, what you have told me. We will talk about this again, late this evening after supper.

Arthur: Ok, father! They all went to the stone again, to watch others try to pull the sword out of the stone, but they all failed. Arthur wondered to himself, how could it have been so easy for him to pull the sword out, when everyone there was a lot stronger than he was.

Later that night after the rest of the village was asleep, Jerry took Arthur and went to where the sword was in the stone. There wasn't anyone else around.

Jerry: Ok son, let's see you pull the sword out of the stone. Arthur catches hold of the sword's handle and it slipped out of the stone.

Jerry: Quick put it back. Arthur did as he was told. Then Jerry tried to pull the sword from the stone but could not budge it.

Merlin had felt the swords release and hurried back to the granite mountain, to see who had pulled the sword from the stone. The camp was starting to wake up, so Jerry and Arthur returned to their camp, again Jerry told Arthur not to tell anyone, what he had done. Jerry needed time to think. This boy was not his real son and he wanted to see one of his sons become King.

Merlin was surprised to see the sword still in the stone when he arrived in camp. He knew that the new ruler had to be there. The crowd met Merlin and asked if he had come to watch them claim the sword.

Merlin: Yes, today is the day, when the new King will pull the sword from the stone and claim the throne. Merlin knew the sword had been released from the stone, but for some reason, had been put back. What was the new King afraid of that he would do this? It made no sense that any of these men would be afraid to become King; it was why they came here. It was nighttime when he felt it being released. It must be either one of the weaker men or one of the boys. They could have sneaked a try during the night, when they were able to pull the sword; they could have thought that someone would hurt them to take it away.

Merlin knew what he must do. He had to let the King know that he would be safe, if he let everyone know who he was, and he had to eliminate who would try to pull the sword, because there was just too many here, for them all to try today.

Merlin: I am here to witness the King pull his sword from the stone. I will remind you that the King and only he can pull the sword out. I can feel that the King is here, so you may start trying after I ask some questions. If you have tried to pull the sword out at least once, move over here. Merlin had pointed to the left and over half the men moved to that area because most of them had been there trying for weeks, even months.

Since Merlin felt the sword being released two nights ago, he knew what his next question would be. Merlin: Everyone who arrived from yesterday morning until now move over here. Merlin pointed to his right and all except 10 men and a couple dozen boys, moved to that area. Merlin smiled because he knew that this was going to be a little easier than he thought.

Merlin: The King is one of those in front of me. Men if you would kindly line up, you will be the first ones to try. As the men lined up, Jerry told Arthur that when the boys tried, he wasn't allowed to because he was too young to be King. Then he lined up with the other men to try, because no one but Arthur knew that he had already tried.

Each one of the men tried with everything that

they had, to pull the sword from the stone but it would not move, not even a little bit. When Merlin told all of the boys to line up, from tallest to shortest, some of the men went to yelling.

First man: How can the King be a boy? He would not be old enough or wise enough, to make the decisions a King would have to make.

Second man: A boy is too weak to protect himself. How would he be strong enough to protect his throne?

Third man: If a boy becomes King he would never have the respect from the countries around us. They would see him, our country, and us as a joke. How would he ever be able, to protect his people from an invasion?

Merlin put up his hands and everyone got silent. Merlin: These are all good questions, so I will enlighten you on a few facts. You asked how he can be wise enough to make decisions a King would have to make. To start with, no great King or Queen has ever made decisions on their own. They have always had trusted advisors to give them several different viewpoints of a situation, and several different solutions. I would be one of those advisors, to help guide him on his way. Second of all, who better than a boy to be King. He would not be filled with lust for wealth and power, as a lot of you already are. Some of the men grumbled under their breath but didn't say anything aloud. Others just dropped their heads in shame, for they knew they were guilty, of at least part of what Merlin had said.

Merlin: As for being strong enough to protect his throne and himself. The sword in the stone is no ordinary sword. Its name is Excalibur and is a magical sword, given as a gift from The Lady of the Lake, which is a very powerful sorceress. She made this sword to help find our next King, who would be honest and pure of heart. How honest are you and how pure is your heart? Who better than a boy, to weld this special sword and be our King, for he hasn't learned the art of deception and would not be corrupted yet? Don't answer these questions but think about them. As you think, also know, that with Excalibur in the King's hand, he cannot be harmed in any way and can't be defeated in battle. Besides, like all the great Kings and Queens before him, he would also have loyal guards to protect him and his throne and I will also protect him.

The men started to understand the wisdom in Merlin's words and started to settle down some more, ashamed that they would doubt any man or boy who pulled the sword from the stone, would be anything but a great King. Merlin: As for others seeing him or us as being a joke. It has been told, that the greatest warriors will come from far and wide to become his knights and help him make this country one of the strongest and most respected, in the whole world. The King will be fair, honest, and just to all in his Kingdom, and we will all thrive because of him. Most of them started shaking their heads yes in agreement because they knew Merlin was a very powerful and wise wizard.

Merlin was pleased that the men were starting to understand that they could not just take or argue their way to the throne. He also hoped that the new King also understood that he would be in no danger by pulling the sword out.

Merlin: As I said before, now all of the boys will line up, from the tallest to the shortest. They will take their turn and try to pull Excalibur from the stone. When the King is revealed, I hope you all are wise enough to show him the respect that he deserves. As the boys started taking their turns, Arthur was at the end of the line, because even though he was tall for his age, he was still a little shorter than the other boys. Jerry walked up and told him again that he was not allowed to try with the other boys. He was just too young to be King. Jerry took Arthur to stand with him and the other men, who had just tried.

Each one of the boys took their turns, including both of Arthur's brothers. Try as they might, none of them could move the sword either. Merlin looked around, confused. He didn't understand why one of the boys wasn't able to pull the sword out. Then he spotted Arthur standing with the men who had tried, Jerry was trying to keep him hidden behind him, but Arthur was peaking around the side of him.

Merlin: Boy, why did you not get in line with the others to take your turn?

Jerry: What boy are you talking to? Merlin in a very stern voice: The boy you are trying to hide behind you. Release him now so he can come to me! Jerry let Arthur go but whispered to him that he was to tell Merlin that he didn't want to try.

Arthur walked up to Merlin with a sad look on his face. Merlin: What is your name boy?

Arthur: My name is Arthur and that is my father, Jerry, that I was standing behind.

Merlin: Are you ready to take your turn, to try to pull Excalibur out of the stone?

Arthur: I can't, father told me to tell you that I didn't want to try. Merlin gave Jerry a very harsh look and then smiled at Arthur.

Merlin: What else did your father tell you?

Arthur: He told me that I was too young to be a King and that I should tell no one that I had already pulled the sword out twice before.

Merlin: Arthur, if you please, will you pull Excalibur out of the stone and show us all, that you are our King.

Arthur didn't hesitate; but walked over to the stone, pulled Excalibur out, and lifted it above his head, so everyone could see his beautiful sword. Merlin went down on one knee: Long live the King, long live King Arthur. Everyone else went down on one knee except Jerry. He walked up to Arthur and put out his hand.

Jerry: Give me the sword and I will be King until you are old enough to rule. Jerry tried to take the sword from Arthur's hand, but Excalibur knocked him backward onto the ground. Merlin ordered some of the men, to hold Jerry where he was. Jerry started yelling at Arthur: It should have been me or one of my sons, to pull the sword from the stone not you. You are nobody. You are just an orphan I found that no one wanted.

Arthur was hurt and confessed, what his father was saying, made no sense. Arthur looked up at Merlin, with tears in his eyes. Merlin in a tender voice: When you pulled Excalibur out of the stone the first time, I had a vision of you as a baby. You are the son of King Edward and Queen Elizabeth, who were killed right after you were born. A castle nursemaid put you in a basket and into the river, to save your life. You floated down the river to safety. A young woman washing clothes at the river, found you and was taking you home with her. On the way home, she got snake bit and died before she could get you somewhere safe. Jerry found you and not knowing that you were now the true and rightful King, took you in and raised you as one of his sons. In my vision, I did not see Jerry's face, so I did not know who saved you, but I did know that it was you who pulled Excalibur out of Father Time's hand.

Jerry's sons both went down on one knee and pledged their allegiance to their adopted brother. All the other men in the crowd also pledged their allegiance to their new King. Jerry felt ashamed of what he had tried to do, also pledging his life and service to the new King. Arthur took the sword Excalibur and went down into the crowd where Jerry was kneeling. Arthur: Father, if you think I am too young, you may be King until you think that I am old enough.

Jerry looked up at Arthur: Son, Excalibur and Merlin both think that you are old enough. They are wiser than I am. I am proud to have you, as my son and as my King.

Merlin: Long live King Arthur! Then they all joined in, saying long live King Arthur! Before all the men left to return to their own villages, they each swore allegiance to their new King.

Merlin took Arthur to an old palace, then told him all about the Queen that used to rule there and all the good she had done. The old palace where Kieris had reined had been destroyed.

Arthur: Merlin, I want to build a new palace on this spot and name it Camelot. I liked her idea, of the round table and knights, to protect the poor and innocent. Help me find the knights and again establish the round table.

So, began the legend of King Arthur.